MOOD I

Once again the prestigiou~~~~ ~~~~~~
Literary Award has produ~~~~ a writer or re-
markable talent.

Mandy Sayer's novel-in-stories, *Mood Indigo*,
explores the less salubrious side of Australian
life mainly from the point of view of Rose,
aged three or four as the novel opens, a
teenager as it ends.

Here are the pubs, the beaches, the cheap
suburbs. What dominates here is a lack of
prospects — except those viewed through the
bottom of a glass.

Yet Mandy Sayer is never sentimental, and
the characters who populate *Mood Indigo* are
entirely credible. There is, literally, music
running through the novel, not only in
Sayer's descriptions of pianos and piano
players, but also in her writing style which
arouses the reader's mind and feelings in
much the way that great music can.

ALLEN & UNWIN
FICTION

Mandy Sayer was born in Sydney on St Valentine's Day at the Marrickville Salvation Army Hospital in 1963. She has studied tap dance and performed in Australia and New York City, and has taught in numerous dance schools and studios. A writer of prose, plays, and poetry, she is currently pursuing a degree in creative writing at Indiana University, where she was awarded the 1989 Myrtle Armstrong Fiction Award, the 1989 Keisler Poetry Award, and the 1989 N.S.A.L. Literature Merit Award for short fiction. Her memoir, *Dreamtime Alice*, was a finalist in the 1988 Australian/Vogel Literary Award. *Mood Indigo* is her first novel.

CONTENTS

For my very best friend, Yusef

1

COOGEE

If you'd asked her how old she was, she would have pulled her thumb out of her mouth and held up four sand-covered fingers. But she knew how to say 'fair dinkum' and 'bloody eh', how to make her father and his circle of muso mates double over with laughter beneath the shade of their bush hats and faded terry towelling caps. 'G'day, mate,' and 'c'mon, fair suck of the sav', brought gentle guffaws and daily gifts of ginger beer and Coogee meat pies with tomato sauce.

'You gunna learn to swim, luv?' asked Laurie Foster, a trumpet player, as he dabbed a lump of zinc cream on her nose one morning.

'Bloody oath.'

'Where you gunna swim to?'

'The moon.'

'The moon —' mused Laurie. 'Whatcha gunna do there, luv?'

She shrugged and looked at her father. 'I'm, um, I'm gunna, I'm gunna wee on the world.'

They all began to chuckle. Laurie shook his head. Her mother looked up from the *Daily Telegraph* and pursed her lips.

'There's no dunny paper up there, you know, luv,' said Roddy Michaels, another piano player.

She swung around and rested her hands on her hips. 'How do *you* know?'

'Roddy did a gig up there last week, didn't you Rod?' piped up her father.

1

'Yeah,' replied Roddy. 'The dough's good but the travelling's a real bugger.'

Every morning they congregated on Coogee. They'd bring down the esky to keep their beers cold and unroll printed towels; they'd sit in one of the stone alcoves that lined the edge of the beach. They called them ovens. They'd lie in the ovens and bake under December's stark and persistent sunlight, and she would clown around her sandcastles, wearing a pair of blue cotton panties with yellow polka dots as each day bleached her hair whiter.

'You gunna learn to swim, luv?' This time it was Roddy.

'Bloody oath.'

'Where you gunna swim to?'

'I'm gunna —' she bit her lip '— I'm gunna swim to the edge.'

'What edge?' asked her father.

'The edge. Like you said. The edge of the world.'

'Where's that?' said Smithy, a trombonist.

'It's —' she pinched the elastic of her swimming costume '— it's just after Taronga Zoo, near Manly.'

'Won't you fall off?'

'Nope.'

'You sure?'

'Yep. No, no —' she looked up at him '— no worries.'

'No *worries*?' Her mother put down the book she was reading. 'Rosie, what does that mean?'

Rose looked at her, at her oiled skin gleaming in the sunlight, at the orange bikini, at her red toenails. 'It means, it means —' She turned in a circle and looked at her father's mates. 'It means... Don't you know, Mum?'

'I know. But do you know?'

Rose jumped into the air. 'No you don't. *I* know.'

'*Do* you?'

'*Do you*?'

Her mother slipped on her sunglasses. 'Len, she's got to learn to swim and she's got to start speaking English.'

'Whaddya think she's speaking, French?'

'I'm serious. She's a real hit down the pub but what about when she starts school?'

Rose edged away from them, to the side of the oven, and pressed her back against the hot stone.

Her father lit up a smoke. 'Don't start pulling all that pommy crap again. She talks like a trooper. Never shuts up. None of all that baby ga-ga, either.'

'That's what I mean,' her mother persisted, 'a trooper. A trooper all right.'

Rose tilted her face up to the sun. They were at it again. Her father groaned and her mother waved a hand in the air. Everything else was warm. The stone, the sun. 'Look, Mum,' she cried, crouching onto the sand. Her mother turned. Rose sprang up and spun around in a circle. She kicked her legs up and flung her arms from side to side. 'I'm a can dancer, see?!' She glided through the oven, across sand, around the white styrofoam esky and her mother's canvas deck chair.

'You mean can-*can* dancer,' said her mother, laughing.

But the real day came when her mother sat down on the deck chair and began blowing up one of two plastic yellow floaties. It wasn't the seaweed she was afraid of. It wasn't that. For she often fancied that it looked like long, thick strands of green hair. And it wasn't the bluebottles. She liked to gaze at the deep aquamarine of their tentacles, would even dance around them when they'd been washed up on the sand.

'You gunna learn to swim, luv?'

She glanced at her father. 'Ask me something else.'

He tilted his hat upwards. 'All right. What's your name?'

'Rose.'

'Rose who?'

'Rose.'

'Yeah, Rose who?'

'*Rose*.' She stamped her right foot onto the sand, exasperated.

'Yes,' said her father, 'but Rose *who*?'

'All right!' she cried, throwing her hands up in the air. 'Rose Who!'

She then marched across to a corner of the oven and began burying her feet in sand. She eyed her mother, who was now starting in on the second floatie.

'Whaddya gunna be when you grow up, Rosie Who?' Smithy asked.

'A man.'

'A man?'

'Yep.'

'Whaddya gunna do when you grow up?'

'I'm gunna, I'm gunna play the piano. Like Dad. I'm gunna get a gig on the moon.' She continued to shovel sand with both hands, was up to her calves in it.

Her father sat down beside her. 'You gunna join the union?'

'Nup.'

'Why not?'

''Cause, 'cause they're a bunch of bludgers.'

Smithy fell back on his towel, laughing. Roddy nearly choked on his lemonade. Her father pulled off his bush hat and propped it upon her head.

'You're a bloody card, aren't you? Where'd you pick that up from?'

'You,' she replied, as the hat slid over her face.

They waited 'til the surf was calm. The floaties felt like big muscles around her arms. Roddy, Laurie, and Smithy wished her luck, told her to 'G'arn and have a go'. They lay back on their elbows to watch as her mother and father walked her across the sand.

White foam frothed around her feet. She remembered saying 'bloody oath' over and over again. She remembered the moon and the edge. She remembered having said that she'd even get as far as China. Bloody oath. Fair dinkum.

'Well, go on,' said her mother. 'Show her.'

'Me?' said her father. 'I came along to watch.'

Her mother crossed her arms. 'Len —'

He sighed. 'Look Rosie. It's like this.'

She watched him make circles with his arms.

'And you do this with your legs.' Her mother began kicking her feet back, running on the spot.

She took a step back and watched them both: his flapping arms, her feet kicking sand up in the air. They were both grinning, like they were trying to convince her how much fun it was. She gazed back at the water slapping a slow rhythm against the shore. In her mind the waves grew big as buildings. She glanced at her parents again, at their limbs stroking the air. She turned and took off across the sand, flinging herself back into the oven, back into the embrace of laughter.

She was wearing Smithy's brown felt swaggy hat. Bottle corks attached to yellow string hung around the brim to keep flies at bay. On Smithy, the corks hung at nose level. On Rose, they brushed against her neck.

'You gunna start school next year, luv?'

'No.'

'Why not?' said Laurie, handing her a Coogee meat pie.

'I wanna stay here. I wanna stay here with you blokes.'

Her father dabbed some tomato sauce on top for her. 'Can't stay here forever.'

'I already been here forever.' She parted the corks so she could take a bite.

'Don't you wanna be like your brother and sister and go off on your own every morning?'

'Can youse come, too?'

'Course not,' replied Smithy.

'Then I'm gunna stay for the rest of forever too, then.'

'Reckon you can last that long?'

She licked around her mouth. 'How long have youse been here?'

Smithy opened a can of beer. 'Oh, forever and ever. Two years, at least.'

Rose scooped a piece of meat out of the pie with her finger. 'Me, too.'

She was stamping her feet against the sand, crying. Her mother stood over her, sliding a floatie up her arm again. Rose tried to pull away, but her mother had a firm grip around her wrist.

Her father and his mates sat in silence. Her hand was slipped through the second floatie and she howled even louder, glancing from Laurie, to Roddy, to Smithy.

'Come on, Nance,' said her father finally. 'Fair go.'

'I'm giving her a fair go.' The floatie was pushed up over her elbow.

'Nance, she's only a kid. A baby. She's not ready.'

Her mother didn't look up. 'I'm trying to *teach* her, Len.'

'Yeah, I know. But she's not ready. She doesn't even like the water.'

Her mother swung around. 'Listen, you dingbat. I'm gunna teach her something that might save her life. Not all the crap you fill her head with.'

'I don't fill her head with crap. I teach her things.'

'Oh, yeah!' cried her mother, letting go of Rose's wrist. She took a few steps towards him. 'How to piss on the moon. That's really going to help her get on in life, eh?'

He was on his feet. Rose backed away. 'I taught her her *name* and, and her *address* and —'

'And what kind of beer to order when you pull into the drive-in bottle shop,' added her mother. 'Oh, that's a beauty, isn't it?'

'Look, just leave her alone. Stop pushing her.'

'Well somebody's got to! You certainly won't. You can't even push yourself!'

She watched her father grab her mother by the arm. Rose backed away another four paces. She began to sweat.

'What's that supposed to mean? Huh?'

'It means —' her mother pulled away '— that all you're ever interested in is fart-arsing around.'

'Bullshit! What do you do all day? Sit behind those sunglasses like Lady Bloody Muck!'

Rose's head began to throb. They were at it again. She wished they wouldn't. Why did this always come back? Why did the yelling always come after the laughing, and the laughing after the yelling? They were getting stuck into each other. They didn't know how to stop. It was too much. It was too hot. And it felt as if their voices were pushing her, pushing her on, nudging her across the sand. 'Hey, youse, look!' Rose cried, suddenly turning. She made a flying motion with her arms as she bounded away like a duck trying to take off and fly. Her feet splashed the foam. A white spray grazed her face. She leapt up and twisted into the air, imitating the sugar plum fairy, floaties arcing into the breeze, toes pointed. And everything was cold as she fell into the salt and darkness, into the icy arm of a rolling green wave.

2

THE LYREBIRD CONSPIRACY

When the time finally came, there was no struggle, no tears. Their mother took their father's hand and they walked down the hall together slowly, as if edging up a church aisle to be married. Ned carried his suitcase, shadowing them from behind, head bowed. Wanda followed, carrying sheet music and an old wooden metronome, Rose was ahead of them, at the front door, ready to open it. But as her parents drew closer, her father's blank face, the deep lines, the inevitability of it all, froze her hand in place, and the journey from her pocket to the door-knob seemed to take a lifetime.

After he had gone, no one talked of it. They would visit him. They could talk on the telephone. It wouldn't be for very long. Rose sat at his piano and closed her eyes, straining to remember, rubbing a single ivory key, as if the very wishing could take them back, could distil time into a single day when they would always lie in the dark and listen for the lyrebird.

It had been a glorious conspiracy. Her father had already dropped Ned and Wanda off at primary school and was driving Rose down the block to the infants school when he pressed down on the accelerator and sailed past the brown doors through which she reluctantly disappeared each morning. He wound down his window and turned the radio up. Violins wavered through the old MG as they sped down Pyrmont Bridge Road and into town.

When he realised he'd made a wrong turn, he drove over the median strip and they both laughed as the car lurched back onto the road.

He yelled out 'G'day!' to a stranger in the street and Rose bounced up and down with the sheer excitement of it. And when he grew bored with driving around looking for a parking spot, he simply steered the car into the Parliament House driveway and parked beside a shiny dark blue Mercedes.

Hand-in-hand, they half-danced through Hyde Park under dappled sunlight, the canopy of green above them like a leafy cathedral, he leaping into the air and she following. They ran in circles. They cartwheeled. He told her to breath in the fresh morning air and she did.

They flopped on their backs beside a bed of poppies and he pointed to the clouds, tracing elephant heads and boats with his finger. She rolled into the crook of his arm and pressed a hand against the stubble of his unshaven face.

'Dad,' she said, 'I love you.' She snuggled in closer. 'Can I marry you when I grow up?'

But he just laughed, pulling away from her, diving into a forward roll across the grass and springing to his feet.

They chased each other around the poppy bed, only to stop on opposite sides, Rose giggling intermittently as they gazed over fiery reds and oranges. She crouched down and plucked one and placed it between her teeth. She circled around the flowers towards him, dancing some ballet that played inside her head, her mouth stretched into a wide grin, the poppy bobbing up and down. She handed it to him with a curtsey and he bowed back, smelling the poppy with an exaggerated sigh.

'Thank you,' he announced, sounding like the queen, and slid the poppy behind his ear so it bloomed beside his left eye. He wiggled his bottom and tried to do the hula, flopping his hands from side to side while she pulled at another flower.

He took her hand and led her into the crowds of Park Street, only stopping at a fruit stall to buy a bag of pears for fifty cents. They wandered down George Street, devouring the ripe pears one after the other, dripping juice on their clothes and not caring. She stopped outside Grace Brothers to look at tall mannequins with long black dresses and strings of pearls. One looked like her mother — wavy blonde hair, slender arms, small bosoms — and she suddenly wondered what her mother would think, what she would do when she found out. But by three-thirty they had already picked up Wanda and Ned from primary school and driven home, and when her mother looked up from her book and asked, 'How was school today, Rosie?' Rose just glanced at her father, and he just gave her a quick wink, and she suppressed a smile and said, 'Good.'

The next morning was the same. After dropping off Ned and Wanda, the car sailed past the brown doors once more and he straightened in his seat and asked, 'Where does Miss Rose wish to be driven to today?'

She thought for a moment and said, 'The bridge. The Harbour Bridge.'

'Right, Miss,' he said, and soon they were gliding above green water, listening to Duke Ellington, while ferries below snaked a path to Manly and Taronga Zoo and white sails freckled the harbour.

'Spiffing!' he cried, as the towering metal arced above them. 'Capital idea, Miss Rose.'

She crouched in her seat and stuck her head out the window into the rush of wind, and when they arrived at North Sydney he turned the car around and went back again, pointing to the radio and saying, ' "All Blues". Miles Davis, live. Recorded in 1964, New York City.' And they crossed the bridge back and forth several times that morning, he handing her a twenty-cent piece each time so she could lean across and pay the toll man.

The next day he took her into town, to a tailor on Clarence Street, and had her pick out material for a suit he was going to have made. He had a big gig coming up, dates in Melbourne and Adelaide. He had to look just right. He had studio sessions and television shows. This was important. She waded through pure wool and pinstripes, greys, and browns, and navy blues, white seer sucker, and tan polyester. The balding tailor, with tape measure looped around his neck, frowned and shook his head when she finally laid a hand on a roll of green and blue tartan and nodded.

Her father said he wanted the sleeves to be extra long and the trouser cuffs extra tight and shelled out extra bills to have it made quickly.

Late September unravelled with wildflowers and lemonade. Each day grew warmer and longer. They picked up his suit and he put it on in the shop, over a crisp white shirt and black bow tie.

'You playing today, Dad?' she asked, as they climbed back into the car.

He straightened his tie and turned the radio on. 'Rosie?' He threw his jeans into the back seat. 'Have you ever heard a lyrebird sing?'

Rose wound down her window. 'No, I don't think so. What's a lie bird?'

'Lyrebird,' he said, turning on the ignition. 'They can sing for twenty minutes and not take a breath.'

Rose glanced at him, trying to decide whether to believe him or not.

'You,' he continued, 'you cannot go through life and not hear it.' And with that, he swung the car around a corner and turned into Market Street.

They cruised up to the Blue Mountains, through thick bushland breaking open into spring. They talked continually, about words, and colours, and when he was a kid. He stopped the car at the side of the road and got out to hug a tree, his arms circling the blue gum as if it were a lost lover.

Rose followed, embracing a jacaranda, her lips meeting the rough bark. Crickets chorused and the air sweated a scent of eucalyptus.

Her father pointed to an anthill as tall as himself, as wide as her bedroom, and said he once knew an old man who lived inside it. The man sold billy cans of boiled water to passing motorists. Her father felt sorry for the man, and the man would invite him into the anthill, and her father would go in, and he'd sit on the old man's army cot and smoke tobacco with him and talk about the code of the road — swaggy talk — until dusk.

When the old man finally died there was a story about him in the *Daily Mirror*. They'd found money under that cot, heaps of it,

11

wrapped up in red cellophane paper and stored in Arnott's biscuit tins.

'Thousands and thousands of quids!' her father exclaimed, walking towards the anthill.

The dry brown dome looked like a single breast rising out of the ground, riddled with patterns of old rain. Rose followed her father around it as a magpie squawked above. The base was cracked, where green tufts of clover clung to the earth and strands of paspalum rose to meet them.

Part of the entrance had fallen in, but her father dug at the earth like a hungry man until there was a hole big enough to slip inside. And he did, leaving Rose to clutch at the buckle of her belt and wonder if he'd ever return.

'Come into my house!' His voice sounded hollow, unreal, as if he were calling through a long tunnel.

She stepped back, wanting to run to the car, and yet to be with him. Santa Claus weeds swayed in the breeze, their little white heads of fluff nodding up and down.

'Enter!' he bellowed again, and her head bent forward, the magpie swooping down as she leaned into the darkness.

He struck a match and the flame sizzled and then settled into a slow burn, illuminating his grinning face, raised eyebrows, the edges of the musty, crumbling cave of earth. She was scared, but she didn't want him to know, so she kept her eyes fixed on the glow of his flushed face and didn't look to see if the army cot was there, or if an old biscuit tin, in haste or neglect, had been left behind.

'Rosie?' he said, still smiling.

She stepped sideways, closer to the opening. 'Yes?'

A spider's web grazed her forehead and she froze.

He took a step towards her, the match burning down to a thin crooked cinder between his fingertips. 'Rosie, this,' he said, 'this is the lesson.'

She clutched at her buckle again. 'The lesson?'

'Yes. The lesson.'

Something scurried behind him, scratching across the dirt. The smile had dropped away and his eyes were wide. She reached out to touch his free hand and the match, holding to its last second, flickered and dropped away.

'Sit down,' he whispered.

She blinked, straining to see him. 'On the ground?'

'Yeah. Come on. I'll sit with you.'

His hand found hers and they dropped onto the dirt.

'Your new suit —' she said.

'Doesn't matter,' he replied, striking another match. 'Hold it, will you?'

Rose crossed her legs. 'Not s'posed to play with matches.'

'You're not playing with them. You're helping me. It's different. See?'

Rose thought for a moment and nodded. She took the match and held it out so he could see as he went through his pockets. She noticed an old red and white cigarette packet by her foot and a rusty, dented can.

'Dad, is this your cubby house?'

He pulled a small container out of his shirt pocket and popped off the lid. 'You could call it that.' He shook something into his hand. 'My cubby house. My castle. My dream home.'

'Can I have one?' She nodded to the little white lolly-looking things in his hand.

'It's my medicine,' he said, palming them into his mouth.

'Can I have one?'

He began to chew. 'It's my medicine.'

'Yes, but can I *have one*?'

He swallowed. 'It makes me better. All better.'

He turned to her and smiled. He blew out the match. She dropped it. She felt his hand around hers as he leaned back and stretched out on the ground. She followed and edged closer to him. The air was cool and smelled raw and earthy, like the wet clay she loved to sink her feet into at the riverside on Uncle Bob's farm.

'Listen!' her father suddenly whispered, his hand tightening around hers. 'Can you hear them? They must be here. They must be very close.'

She closed her eyes and listened.

'Can you hear them?'

She tightened her face. She held her breath. She listened harder.

'They're singing. Hear that?' he whispered into her ear. 'They're singing. Just for us. Hear that high note there? C sharp. Beautiful. D. Yes, F sharp. Perfect. F sharp. Perfect. Perfect, perfect pitch.'

She shifted closer to him and slung an arm across his chest. She blinked at the darkness and squeezed her eyes shut. She felt his heart beating under her outstretched hand, and for a moment, as his fingers stroked her hair, she thought she could hear it, in the distance, a voice spiralling in trills, singing higher and higher, just for them.

On Saturdays, her mother dressed them up in their Sunday best — Rose almost consumed by crimson satin and frills, a hand-me-down from Wanda. They boarded a green bus that rumbled all the way to Rozelle. Each stop brought them closer to him. Rose would try to count the stops, to keep track of progress, only to lose it as they veered into Balmain Road and the flurry in her stomach, the anticipation of seeing him, was too much.

Wanda read aloud every sign or word painted in black inside the bus. *Please pay conductor. No smoking. Do not stand beyond this point*, she chimed, turning in her seat to find something new.

Ned swung Rose up into the air and let her pull the cord, and she hung on, pulling it again and again, loving the sound of the echoing *dong*, until passengers began to click their tongues and her mother pulled on the hem of her dress.

They got off at the main gates and followed a concrete path. Ned and Wanda ran ahead, trying to trip each other, while Rose nervously clutched a yellow pear that she would give to him, that he would eat, that would suddenly make him better.

Inside, the building smelt of bleach, of chlorine, like a deep blue swimming pool. White uniforms glided by and chrome doorknobs glinted under fluorescent light.

They found his bed freshly-made, creaseless. The Chinese man with whom he shared the room sat in the corner, banging a teaspoon against the screen of an unplugged television set.

Rose looked at the untouched bed again. His clothes were gone, his tortoiseshell comb, his metronome and sheet music.

'Upstairs,' said the nurse. 'Third floor. We moved him.'

Rose pressed her fingertips against the pear and followed the lilac flowers on her mother's silk dress into the corridor. Nothing had been the same since the day of the anthill. Nothing ever would be. A letter had come from the school. Her mother had slapped him across the face. A doctor had arrived in a pale blue suit and had sat in the loungeroom, clicking the top of a ballpoint pen with his thumb, up and down.

After walking up a flight of stairs, they found him in a room by himself, sitting on the edge of the bed. The old wooden metronome was positioned in the centre of a portable table directly before him. He slouched, watching the metronome's metal arm tick from side to side, his eyes following the tiny arc it made in the air.

Thick, rusty bars masked a square window overlooking an overgrown garden, a stream, and a red oriental bridge.

They stood in the open doorway, watching him, but he didn't look up, didn't see them, or didn't want to. His eyes just moved back and forth in time, fingers occasionally lifting and dropping against his knees, a silent chord.

Their mother raised a hand to her mouth and turned away, disappearing into the corridor. Wanda followed, quick footsteps growing fainter. Ned leaned against the door-jamb, crossing his arms. And Rose, not knowing what to do, smoothed down her crimson satin and walked towards him.

She cupped the pear in her hands and held it out to him. He didn't see it, his eyes still arcing from side to side. She lifted one of his hands and pressed the pear into it, closing each finger around ripe, yellow flesh.

'Dad?' she said, glancing out the window, through the bars, into the garden. A willow tree rustled in the wind, long strands of green waving up at her. Daisies bowed into the breeze, and petals fluttered away from a thick rose bush.

'Dad?' Her voice fell to a whisper. 'Can you hear them? Can you hear them, Dad?'

She sat down on the bed and leaned against him. 'They must be very close. Listen! C sharp. D. F sharp. Remember?' She touched his cheek. 'C sharp. D. F sharp. Beautiful. Can you hear them? Can you hear them, Dad?'

He didn't look up. He said nothing. But she was sure she saw him smile as his eyes ticked back and forth, was sure he nodded at the metronome and made a sound. She was so sure of this that she curled up on the bed beside him and listened, listened hard, and waited for the lyrebird's perfect stolen song.

3

BURRUNGURRULONG HOTEL

It was between Emu Plains and the Blue Mountains, where every-thing remains a dusty brown before giving in to a violet shadow of early foothills. It was a big brick thing on a street with only a butcher shop, a milk bar, and another pub. Aunty Mag dropped them off at the door, told them to keep in touch, and sped off down the street in her old VW beetle, the exhaust pipe held in place with a dirty black and gold Balmain footy sock.

Rose turned in a circle. 'This is it?'

Her mother looked around and nodded. She steered Rose and her sister, Wanda, away from a line of men sitting on the steps of the bar, drinking, and led them around to the side where a large verandah with white pillars and cane chairs sprawled out to meet them.

The door opened and a huge great dane leapt out, barking. Rose grabbed her mother's arm. Wanda jumped back. A dark-haired woman in a pink satin housecoat stood in the doorway crying, 'Samson! Come here. Heel!' She clutched her coat at the neck with one hand and grabbed the dog's collar with the other. 'Good morning, Mrs Partridge,' she continued, yanking the dog back. 'These must be your daughters. Come in.' The dog danced about as she ushered them into a long red-carpeted hallway with a high ceiling. Rose eyed the dog: he seemed as big as a lion, almost as tall as her. Lean, long-legged, and muscular, his silver-grey fur fitted him like a tailored suit.

Her mother introduced them. The woman held onto the dog's collar and smiled down at Rose and Wanda. The woman was wearing pink lipstick but not all the other stuff women put on their faces. She had brown eyes and a beauty spot on the left side of her mouth. Rose remembered what her mother had said about the woman and the man and their kids, remembered what she was supposed to do, and suddenly smiled back.

The woman said her name but Rose had forgotten it by the time they had reached the top of the stairs. The woman showed them two small rooms — one for the two girls, one for their mother — that overlooked the dry and empty main street.

She said that the boys wouldn't be home for a few hours and Rose was glad of that. Boys were a part of life that had to be tolerated like cod liver oil and school uniforms. Except for Ned, of course. But Ned was gone. Gone to live with Uncle Bob on the farm. But not for long. Just a while. Just a bit. Just 'til her father got better.

The boys, she thought. There were three of them. The woman spouted off their names and smiled again. She looked at Rose and Wanda and said she knew they were all going to get along fine. Just fine. Then there was a pause and nobody said anything; just the sound of the dog's panting breath filled the room.

Rose found herself downstairs in a big, carpeted kitchen with three refrigerators. Her mother was bustling between the pantry and the stove, a white apron already hanging around her neck and tied at the waist. The woman had said, 'Please don't bother today, you can start tomorrow'. But her mother was eager to please. She told Rose to stand up straight, to be nice, to smile. Rose propped herself on a green vinyl swivel chair and rehearsed this, her arms folded on top of the white laminex table. Her blonde hair was pulled up into a tight bun like her mother's and sprayed with lots of VO5. This was her mother's idea. She'd look neat and respectable. She'd look like a girl. Rose thought it made her round face look even fatter, while her hair felt like strips of cardboard.

She was young enough to believe that babies were born from

kissing and old enough to know she wanted to be an actress. She practised smiling, crossing her legs, imagined herself greeting the woman and her dog with a gracious bow. In her mind, big black film cameras appeared in each corner of the kitchen. Her mother was in it too, of course, but she was the star. Light flooded the room and someone ran up to powder her nose. She sat up straight and smiled. She tilted her face up to meet the powder puff.

Her mother put the kettle on for a cuppa. She turned to Rose and asked, 'Do you think they'd like Milo?'

Rose swivelled the chair around to meet her mother's gaze. The cameras were still humming along. She stood up and bowed. 'Yes, Mother. I do think they would like Milo.' She bowed again and sat down, swivelling her chair back around.

There was a pause. Her mother walked across to the table. 'Now don't you go bunging on an act, Rose. Just be normal. You hear me? Just be normal.'

'You told me to be nice.'

'That's right. Nice. Normal. Sit up straight. Be nice *and* normal, all right?'

Rose nodded. Her mother went back to the stove.

'I normally don't sit up straight.'

Her mother stopped suddenly and turned. 'I don't have time for all this silly talk.' She pointed a teaspoon at Rose. 'Be nice, normal, sit up straight, and smile. Got it?'

'Got it.'

'Good.'

Her mother stood two pink teacups and saucers on the stove.

'I don't know if they really would like Milo,' said Rose.

'But you said —'

'I was just being nice.'

Her mother lifted the whistling kettle from the stove. 'All kids like Milo.'

Rose drew a circle on the laminex with her finger. 'I like tea.'

'Yes, dear. I know.'

After pouring the boiled water into a bone china teapot, her mother popped on a woollen cosy and turned the pot anti-clockwise three times.

Rose jumped as she heard the front door slam and dogs begin to bark. She sat up straight and smiled at the wall. Her mother hitched up her apron and tightened the bow. Rose uncrossed her legs. Her mother gave the teapot another turn.

'Hello,' said a boy who had stopped in the doorway. Rose looked him over. He was about six, perhaps. He had straight brown hair with a fringe and big brown eyes like his mother's. He was chubby, too. The kid was a real tub.

'Hello,' replied Rose and her mother in unison.

The boy held onto his plastic schoolcase and regarded them. Rose felt awkward. She was in his kitchen, sitting on his chair, at his table.

'Now, which one are you?' Her mother walked across the kitchen and took his schoolcase. She rested her hand on his shoulder and ushered him to the table. He slid onto a swivel chair across from Rose.

'Leon,' he replied, looking down at the laminex.

'Leon,' said Rose, 'is that short for Leonardo? Like, Leonardo der Vinci?'

Her mother shot her a glance.

The boy pursed his lips. 'Just Leon.'

'Well, my name's Nancy,' said her mother, 'and this is Rose.'

'I thought there was another one,' murmured Leon.

'Another what?'

Leon shifted in his chair. 'Girl.'

'Oh, you must mean Wanda. She's upstairs. Would you like me to go and —'

'No,' said Leon.

'Would you like some Milo?'

The front door slammed again and the dogs barked once more.

'No.'

'Or some tea? I just made some —'

Rose looked up to see another two standing in the doorway. They were older, bigger. Rose forgot to smile and simply stared at them. The smaller one was about nine or ten. He had the same haircut as Leon but was blond and had blue eyes. He wasn't a tub and the taller one was just plain skinny. The skinny one was fair also, but his hair was more short-back-and-sides, more like a grown-up. Rose noticed his down-turned mouth and began to slouch.

'Hello!' said her mother, trying to sound bright. 'My name's Nancy. What's yours?'

The taller boy leaned against the door jamb. 'Count Dracula.'

The younger one chortled and her mother forced out a laugh. 'That's very funny. And you?' She turned to the younger one.

'Elvis Presley,' he replied, giving his hips a quick wiggle.

Leon sighed and pointed a finger at the older one. '*He's* Lance. And him,' Leon continued, nodding at the younger one, 'he's Lester.'

'People call me Lucky,' added the boy.

Rose looked at them both. They were going to be a pain in the neck, him with his wiggly hips and the other one looking back at her like she was a dead fish.

'All these L's!' declared her mother, slipping her hands into her apron pockets. 'Lance, Lucky, and Leon. Well, I think that's lovely.' She gave a quick laugh and looked from one to the other, as if wondering what to say next.

Lucky slowly crossed his arms and frowned. 'You won't last, you know,' he said finally.

Her mother's eyebrows rose. 'I beg your pardon?'

'That's right,' said Lance, taking a step forward, his skinny arms hanging at his sides, hands clenched. 'None of 'em ever do. Two weeks. Two months.' He looked her mother straight in the eye and crossed his arms also. 'No longer than two months. None of 'em ever do.'

'Yeah,' added Lucky.

'Yeah,' echoed Leon.

Rose slouched a little further. Her mother stepped back; her hand reached for the tin of Milo.

After the boys had wolfed down a tray of anzac biscuits, Leon volunteered to show Rose the stables. At the end of the hallway he opened a door and the carpet changed from red to blue. He walked her through his family's flat and in the livingroom she slowed down to take everything in. The room was bathed in a blue haze and refractions of light that were cast from a tiered chandelier. Above a wide fireplace hung an equally large mirror with a gold, gilt-edged frame. Two deep red waratahs stood in an oriental vase on the mantelpiece. Rose slowly turned in a circle. A blue velvet chaise-lounge sat across on the other side of the room by the wall. Her eyes looked up to find a painting of a woman. Rose blinked. The woman didn't have any clothes on. Rose glanced at the chaise-longue again and then back at the painting. She took three steps closer. Brown hair fell across white breasts. The woman was lying on the chaise-longue and staring out into the room.

'She's beautiful, isn't she?' said Leon.

Rose stared at the curve of her hips, her alabaster skin. But the beauty spot had moved. In the painting it was on her right cheek, parallel with the tip of her nose.

'That's your mum,' said Rose.

Leon nodded. 'I know. Come on.' He walked to a glass door that led onto the veranda. 'I'll show you War and Peace and Passionfruit and, and Gundagai Gerty. There's also Lady Chatterly and there's the pool, too.'

He opened the door and Rose stepped through.

They wandered down a path by a bed of withered sunflowers and a kidney-shaped pool dotted with dead leaves. Leon opened a wooden gate at the end of the path and they both walked onto cracked dry earth sprinkled with straw.

Rose found herself directly facing the backside of a white horse. A blonde tail swished back and forth, shooing away flies. The smell of manure was heavy. The horse turned around to meet them.

'This is Fay's Fantasy,' said Leon.

'What?'

'Fay's Fantasy. It's his name. He's our best horse. Dad's got a special thing he feeds 'em now. Makes 'em run fast. He was in the paper about it before. In the *Tele*.'

They walked around the horse and Leon climbed through the fence that bordered between stables.

Rose climbed through also. 'What's he feed 'em?'

'He never says. It's a, a secret. Sumpin' about eggs. He was just in the paper about it. His picture, too.'

Rose nodded. She gazed at a dark brown horse slowly walking into its stable. Somewhere in the back of her mind the cameras clicked on and the theme song of *National Velvet* rose up around her. 'Do you ever get a ride on them?'

Leon shook his head. 'Dad says they're race horses. Thorough-breds. Not shetland ponies.'

'I'd like to ride one,' she said, eyeing a grey horse pulling at some straw in the corner of the next stable. The music grew louder. She imagined herself in a red and white satin racing uniform, with riding cap and boots.

Leon shook his head. 'Nup. Thoroughbreds. Dad said so.' Leon drew an 'L' in the dust with the heel of his shoe. 'We're only allowed near 'em to give 'em a carrot or some sugar.'

Leon took her through the remaining stables and introduced her to Lady Chatterly and Passionfruit, War and Peace, and Gundagai Gerty, and another tan-coloured horse named Power Without Glory. After they had slipped back through the series of fences and reached the wooden gate, Rose turned and looked at the white horse once more.

'Leon?' she began, watching the horse bow his head to the water trough.

'Yeah?'

'Who's Fay?'

'Fay?' said Leon.

'Yes.'

'Fay's my mum.'

Rose crossed her arms and looked back at the horse. 'Can we see the pub?'

'Now?'

Rose nodded.

Leon turned towards the gate. 'Not now. The place is choc-a-bloc. Wait 'til Sunday. I'll show you on Sunday.'

As they walked back down the path they saw Lance and Lucky kicking around a soccer ball by the pool.

'Got a bloody sheila now, Leon, eh?' said Lance.

Lucky ran towards the ball. 'Didja take her down the stables and give her a root?'

'Shut up,' retorted Leon.

23

They kicked the ball between each other, working their way closer to the path. Rose thought a root was what kept flowers standing in soil, much the same as feet. Lucky gave the ball one swift kick and it shot towards her and bounced off her forehead.

'Nice shot!' cried Lance.

The ball hit the ground and Rose ran after it. She swiped it up as Lucky went to kick. He lost his balance and fell backwards onto the grass and Rose tossed the ball into the pool.

'Whadja do that for?' said Lance, shoving her.

'Yeah!' added Lucky, picking himself up.

'You, you hit me in the head.' She stepped back. 'You coulda given me brain damage.'

'You already got brain damage,' snarled Lucky, poking her in the stomach with his index finger.

Rose pushed him away. '*You* have.'

'What happened to your father?' Lucky craned his head forward and smirked. 'Didja mother shoot him?'

'Shut up.'

'Did she stab him with a knife?'

Rose shoved him again.

'Did she poison him and put him in the freezer?'

Rose felt Lucky's hand tighten around the collar of her dress. She held her breath. His fingers dug into her neck. She grabbed him by the arm.

'Did she cut off his dick? Did she stuff him? Did she?'

'Shut up!'

'*Did* she?'

Rose wrenched him back and then shoved him forward, but he didn't loosen his grip on her dress and she went sailing into the pool with him. All was quiet under the water except for a mumble of rising bubbles. All was pale blue. Her clothes loosened around her skin. She felt weightless.

'What in God's name has got into you?' demanded her mother. Her voice was like a slap across the face. She didn't believe in spanking kids but this was just as bad. Rose was standing by the wardrobe in her room. She looked down at her wet sneakers and saw she was dripping onto the carpet.

'What did I tell you, Rose? What did I tell you?' She grabbed Rose by the shoulders and shook her, as if an answer might fall out of her mouth like a peach from a tree. 'I told you to behave! Didn't I?' Another shake. 'Didn't I?'

'Y-yes.'

'And what do you do?' Her mother let go and paced across the room. 'You go and push one of them in a *pool*? On our first day here?' Her mother swung around. 'Do you want to get me fired?'

Rose shivered. Lucky had bunged on an act and started bawling when he saw his mother. Lance stood by and backed up his brother's story. Leon had said nothing.

'Huh?'

'No.'

'Listen young lady,' her mother paced back towards her, 'you're going to have to straighten up very fast. No more smart-alec remarks and no more nonsense.'

'But he —'

'I don't want any excuses. You be nice to those boys. They're nice boys. Do you hear?'

Rose touched the wet hem of her dress. All she could see was Lucky's jeering expression, a top lip raised to bare teeth. She glanced at Wanda, at the mane of fair hair falling across her shoulders, at the way she sat on the bed smiling to herself: it was Rose who was copping it for a change.

'Do you?' Her mother shook her again.

'Yes, Mum.'

'All right. Now get out of those wet things and go and have a bath.' Her mother straightened her apron and left the room.

Downstairs, the dogs started up a litany of barks. Wanda stood on her bed and sticky-taped a poster of Rick Springfield to the wall. Rose began unbuttoning her dress.

'Wan?' she said.

'Yeah?'

'It wasn't my fault.'

Wanda bit the tape with her teeth. 'Sure, Rose.'

'It wasn't!'

'I bet.'

Rose glared at her sister, at the tight Levis and the Rolling

Stones T-shirt. She'd already changed outfits three times that day.

'Not you, too.'

'What?' Wanda took a step back on the bed. The poster was crooked.

'You like 'em.'

'Who?'

Rose stepped out of her dress. 'The boys.'

'I hardly even spoke to 'em.'

'I know.'

'Well?'

'Well what?'

'Well, what are you talking about?'

Rose reached for her towel. 'Nothing.'

'Well that's true,' said Wanda, straightening the poster. 'That's all you ever talk about.'

Rose wandered along the red hall in her dressing gown and Mickey Mouse slippers. Five doors down she found the word *Ladies* painted in black on frosted glass. She pushed open the door and found a bathroom lined with white, triangular tiles and blue trim. It looked like the inside of a restroom at an old railway station and smelt like Pine-O-Cleen. There were six toilets and two baths. The plugs were chained to the taps.

She shut the door of one cubicle and turned on the water full blast. An inch-wide cake of Lux lay in the soap dish wrapped in waxy paper. She tore it open and tossed the tiny wafer into the water.

She turned it all over in her mind. She was going to be good from now on. She was going to shut up. They needed this. It was better than staying out at Aunty Mag's place, with all her kids, at the Housing Commission flats. It was better than hanging around the Smith Family office and asking for boxes of tinned foods every week. It was better than going through the donation bins. It was. Her mother had said that they were lucky, and they were. They were lucky. She was going to shut up from now on.

Rose dragged her hand through the bathwater and stepped out of her slippers. She pulled on the bow at her waist and let her dressing gown drop to the floor. She lifted one leg over the side of the bath and thought she heard something, a giggle, perhaps. She turned off the tap and swung around. A pair of upside-down faces peered through the foot-long gap between the bottom of the door and the floor. It was Lance and Lucky, their laughter amplified by the bathroom's white emptiness.

Mr Taylor had called a house meeting that night and everyone had filed into the kitchen. The boarders — five men who worked for the Department of Main Roads — sat at the table; Jackie, the Irish horsetrainer, leaned against one of the refrigerators; the boys sat on the countertop; Wanda and Rose stood by their mother at the stove.

Mrs Taylor floated in like a pink cloud. She was wrapped in pale chiffon, an evening dress edged with silver sequins. Mr Taylor followed. Rose had been wondering about him. They'd been at the hotel all day and still hadn't met him. She expected him to be tall and blond, like the two older boys, and was surprised to see an overweight, greying man with a red face lumber into the room. It seemed as if he had barely squeezed into his black dinner suit and Rose stood there wondering how he had managed to do his buttons up.

'Right-o, this won't take long.' Mr Taylor scanned the room. Rose noticed his yellowing teeth. 'We've only got a few things to discuss so let's get on with it. Everybody, this is the new house-keeper, Nancy.' Mr Taylor gestured to Rose's mother. 'And her two kids. So if you've got any problems you go and see Nancy now, OK?'

Her mother smiled at everyone. She opened her mouth to say something.

'Now the next thing is this,' continued Mr Taylor, 'the dogs are in heat. OK? Everyone understand?' No one said anything. 'And we're trying to mate Samson and Delilah, see?'

He slid his hands into his pockets. Rose crossed her arms. What did this mean?

'We're trying to get Sam and Del together 'cause they're both a good breed, see? Knock out a good litter together, those two. The best. The best in Australia, anyway. Great danes are meant to be just that. Great.'

Still no one said anything. It was Mr Taylor talking. It was the boss. Jackie rubbed his beard and nodded. One of the DMR blokes crossed his legs.

'Not like that bitch, Cleopatra. See, she's no good. She's the wrong colour, she's black, and she's too small. Doesn't look right. Her papers aren't the best, either.'

Mr Taylor paused and looked around the room. 'What I'm trying to *say* is that we don't want Samson to mate with Cleo! We want him to do it with Del, right?'

Everyone looked at each other and nodded.

Mr Taylor ran a hand across his wavy, oiled hair. 'Now the problem is this, fellas. Think about it, two hot females in heat and only one Samson. Think about it.'

Another pause. Rose heard her mother clear her throat, but nothing was said. Jackie smirked. Mrs Taylor nudged her husband, almost a smile playing on her lips.

'Well it's as simple as this,' he continued. 'The two bitches are gunna tear each other apart. I know. It's happened before. That Cleo's a real dingo. She'd have Delilah for breakfast. So this is what we're gunna have to do —' Mr Taylor paused and took his wife by the arm — 'Fay and I have decided to put Sam and Del in the yard while they do their thing and Cleo stays locked in the pen down near the stables, see?'

Everyone nodded.

'And I don't want those bloody dogs tramping through the house while they're in heat. Make sure they stay out in the yard.' Mr Taylor glanced at the boys and then at Rose and Wanda. 'OK?' Rose found herself nodding while a murmur of agreement rippled through the kitchen.

'Good,' declared Mr Taylor. 'Nothing worse than a couple of bitches in heat sinking their teeth into each other. Right,' he continued, 'the third thing is this. The horses. No more bloody extra carrots and sugar cubes. I know you kids are slipping them extra food every bloody time you go down there and it's gotta stop.' Mr Taylor frowned. 'I bloody well mean it this time! Fay's got a big race coming up and I'm not gunna have her come plodding in last 'cause you kids couldn't stop shovelling food into her. You hear me?' He glared from Lance to Lucky to Leon. The boys nodded.

'Right-o. That's all.' Mr Taylor drew his hands out of his pockets and nodded a goodbye. No one moved until Mrs Taylor had swept out of the room and the large black figure of her husband had disappeared around the door.

The main lounge in the pub stank with stale cigarette smoke and beer. Blue plastic chairs crouched beside round, imitation wood tables. Some chairs were tipped backwards; one was upside down on the bar. Leon and Rose padded across purple carpet blemished with cigarette butts and the odd empty glass. It was like being at a fairground after everyone had gone home.

The lounge seemed as big as a playground, as big as a footy field. Racing pages were strewn across the floor near the cash register. Below a shelf of whiskey behind the bar hung a sign: A *Pill in Time Saves Nine*, with a cartoon of a tiddly woman guzzling from a glass of beer.

Leon stopped at the bar. He bent over and stared at the carpet.

'Look!' He was pointing to a twenty-cent piece lying beneath a stool.

'There's a two!' Rose's hand was swooping down.

Leon crawled along a little further. 'Here's another one.'

Rose jumped ahead of him. 'Here's a five. A five-cent piece and a paper clip.'

Leon crawled around the pool table while Rose nosed under the dart board. Sometimes her hand or knee met a patch of moist carpet still wet with spilled beer, while her fingers uncurled to pocket lost coins that could later buy a bag of lollies or a chocolate heart.

'Dumb drunkies,' said Leon, standing up. 'Lose half their dough. Come on,' he continued, turning, 'let's search the bar. They drink more in there.'

The floor was tiled in the bar. A shattered glass lined the countertop. A half-empty bottle of vodka sat on top of the cash register. 'Leon?' said Rose, picking up a beer gun. 'What does Burru, Burrung, um —'

'Bur-rung-gur-ra-long,' sounded Leon.

Rose squeezed the gun. 'Bur-rung —'

'Gur-ra-long.'

'Gur-ra-long,' repeated Rose. 'Burrungurralong.' She squeezed the gun a little harder. 'What does it mean?'

Leon held up a twenty-cent piece. 'Watering hole.'

Rose squeezed even harder. She held it up. A few drops of beer dribbled out of the gun and splattered on her dress.

Her mother had baked a few chickens, boiled some peas and potatoes, mixed up some Gravox, and began delivering platters to various parts of the hotel. The boarders got the formal dining room; Mr and Mrs Taylor had their food delivered on a silver tray to their bedroom door; the kids got the kitchen. Wanda was picking up peas one at a time and dropping them into her mouth. Lucky mashed his potato with a fork and dolloped on a lump of butter. Leon was slurping up gravy through a crazy straw. Lance peeled off a layer of fatty chicken skin and flung it into the air. It landed on top of the ceramic gollywog salt and pepper shakers.

'Eat it,' he said to Rose. 'It'll make you even fatter.'

Rose put down her fork.

'Yeah, it might give you some tit,' added Lucky, 'like Wanda.'

'Get lost,' Rose murmured, looking down at her food.

'You wouldn't know,' said Wanda, picking up another pea, 'what to do with a tit if you came face to face with one.'

Rose relaxed a little. Wanda could handle them. She'd been hanging out with new friends and had started bringing home all kinds of smart comebacks.

'I'd suck it for some milk,' replied Lucky, plunging his fork into a chicken breast.

'Baby!' said Rose.

'Baby!' said Wanda.

'Baby! echoed Leon.

'Well, if I'm a baby,' sneered Lucky, turning, 'you're a poof.'

Leon put down the straw. His big brown eyes rolled downwards and his mouth drooped.

'Yep, he's a poof all right,' agreed Lance. 'Gutless wonder. Plays with the girls and can't even root 'em.' Lance began to laugh. 'Poor old Lee-Lee the poof boy.'

'Poor old Lee-Lee,' added Lucky, 'the baby poof. The poofta baby. Wait 'til we tell Dad.'

'I'm not a poof!' whined Leon.

'Are,' jeered Lucky. 'You are so.'

'Dickless dag,' said Lance, pushing back his chair and looking around the room as if he were about to part with a precious secret. 'Betcha can't do this, poof boy,' he continued, standing on the chair. Rose looked up to see his long, skinny body towering above the table. He suddenly pulled down his shorts. Rose swallowed. Sticking out above the elastic of his underpants was a pink finger of flesh pointing to the ceiling.

When Rose walked down the path, he wouldn't look at her: no more shared Big Charlies after school, no more hunting for change together in the pub on Sunday morning. Instead Leon took to kicking around a soccer ball and pissing on a pink rose bush near the pool. Rose stopped by the gate and fixed her eyes on Cleo, on the wire fence hemming her into a corner of the yard. Rose turned and walked back down the path.

When she stood by the pool and gazed at Leon, he wouldn't look up. He stood by the bush and killed ants with the heel of his shoe. He cupped his hand over a whole rose and crushed it with one squeeze. He could throw petals into the air like confetti and laugh, but he couldn't look at her.

Rose walked up the steps and onto the veranda. She opened the glass door and slid through, careful not to let Samson and Delilah in as they bounded up behind her.

She sat in the kitchen and nibbled toast and vegemite. Light cut through the closed window as her mother stood at the countertop and sliced kangaroo meat for Mrs Taylor's siamese cat. Rose imagined scores of wild kangaroo being slaughtered to feed Mrs Taylor's 'little princess'.

The cat was meowing and rubbing up against the ankles of Rose's mother. A pot of pea soup boiled over and the kettle began to whistle.

'Oh, shut *up!*' cried her mother. She slammed down the knife and gave the cat a shove with her foot.

Rose jumped up and turned off the gas. She lifted the kettle and poured boiling water into the teapot. She turned it anti-clockwise three times.

'Nancy?' It was Mrs Taylor in the doorway. She had on a blue and gold kimono untied around the waist. Her closed hands overlapped across her chest and kept the cloth in place. 'We'll need the champers at six, along with the prawns.'

Her mother picked up the knife again. 'Yes, Mrs Taylor.'

'Could you make sure it's chilled?'

Her mother drove the knife into meat. 'Yes, Mrs Taylor.'

'And the prawns, too?'

Her mother swung around. 'Everything will be chilled, washed, peeled, polished, pressed and, and punctual.'

Mrs Taylor drew the kimono closer to her neck. 'Thank you.'

After the cat had been fed and the dogs had been served and the horses had received their special formula, her mother washed and skinned duck while Rose sat down to shell prawns.

She picked up a pink shiny body, and a pair of eyes like two black dots made with a texta colour stared back at her.

Sorry Mr Prawn, she mouthed, and suddenly tore off its head with one quick pull. Next came the tail; she took it between her thumb and index finger and the transparent armour came away in her hand.

'Party tonight, Mum?'

Her mother pushed a wad of stuffing into the duck and nodded.

'Another one?'

'Yes.'

'Why do they have so many?'

'Because —' her mother scooped up another handful '— because they're happy.'

'Are they?'

'Yes.'

Rose licked her thumb and tasted the salty residue. 'They got lots of friends.'

'*Have.*'

'What?'

Her mother turned. 'They *have* lots of friends.'

'Yes, I know,' said Rose. 'Lots. Lots and lots and lots.'

Her mother began painting melted butter over the duck with a brush. Rose picked up another prawn.

'How do you suppose they got so many friends?' Rose wondered aloud. She was having trouble at her new school and thought there was some secret she didn't know about.

'Probably bought them.'

'What?'

Her mother wiped her hands on a tea towel. 'Nothing, Rosie.'

Rose put down the prawn. 'They *bought* them?'

'No. No, Rose,' replied her mother. 'I meant, I said caught. They caught them.' Her mother let out a quick, nervous laugh. 'It's hard to catch a good friend these days.'

She lifted the large enamel baking dish and slid the duck into the oven. Then she took a wooden spoon and stirred the soup. It was unusually quiet. The dogs weren't barking and the boys weren't around; Wanda was off with her new friends, and the cat, now satisfied, curled up on the floor within a beam of sunlight and fell asleep.

'I wonder,' mused Rose, 'I wonder why they always stay in their bedroom?'

'Who?'

'Mr and Mrs Taylor.'

Her mother picked up a sponge and began wiping down the oriental vase. 'They come out sometimes, Rose.'

'No they don't. They never do. Only for parties.' Rose snapped off another prawn head. She pulled at the tail and let it drop. She made sure her mother wasn't looking and popped the shelled prawn into her mouth. She chewed and swallowed with only a discreet glance at her mother and wiped her hands on her school uniform. 'They probably,' she said finally, 'they probably watch telly in there all day, eh Mum?'

'Yes, Rosie, they probably do.'

She leaned on the table and rested her chin in her hand. 'I wonder if it's colour or black and white?' She picked up another prawn. 'Probably colour.' She paused and stared at a distorted image of her face reflected in the side of the toaster. Her eyes were too big and her mouth was all squashed up. 'But how do they go to the toilet?' she added, watching her lips move.

'What?'

'Mr and Mrs Taylor.' She looked up at her mother. 'If they never come out of their bedroom, how can they wee?'

'Rose, really! That's enough. Enough of all this silly talk. Shell the prawns, will you?'

Rose went back to her chore reluctantly, still wondering if perhaps Mr and Mrs Taylor kept a potty under their bed and only emptied it in the middle of the night while everyone else was asleep.

'You haven't drunk your tea,' said Rose, eyeing the full teacup beside her own empty one.

Her mother dropped a bunch of gladioluses into the oriental vase. 'No time.'

'I can't drink any more.'

'That's fine.'

Rose fingered a hard, thin prawn shell. 'I will if you want me to.'

'No, that's fine, Rose,' said her mother. 'Here,' she continued, walking across to the table. 'You can take this into the livingroom and put it on —'

'The mantelpiece?'

'Yes.'

'All right.' Rose slid off the chair and placed her palms around the smooth hips of the vase.

She looked up to see her mother bending over to kiss her on the forehead, but the smell of her mother's breath, heavy with the stench of whiskey, made Rose pull away.

Rose came downstairs to the Saturday morning smell of frying bacon and percolated coffee. She could hear the sing-song of Jackie's voice rising and falling in an animated cadence. The kettle whistled and Lance was demanding to know where the tomato sauce was.

She stood in the hall and contemplated walking into the kitchen. She would eat toast and honey. The boys would harass her. Jackie would do a coin trick and find a twenty cent piece behind her ear. She'd have to scrape their dishes when they'd finished. After everything was cleaned up, her mother would sit down with a glass ashtray and smoke three cigarettes in a row.

Rose passed the kitchen doorway and continued down the hall. She'd visit the horses instead, pat them, give them a carrot. They didn't give orders and she didn't have to clean up after them.

As she wandered through the Taylor's apartment, Rose began to tread lightly. Even though she was allowed to walk through on her way to the yard, she always felt like an intruder, a burglar stalking across the carpet. She imagined that they might think she would steal something, would pocket a tiny china ornament, a pack of cards, or the fountain pen that always sat on the oak writing table. She was sure Mrs Taylor looked at her strangely sometimes, was sure that Mrs Taylor suspected her of some small crime and would one day burst out and accuse her of breaking the oriental vase or pinching one of the glass-blown figurines.

Rose tiptoed past Mr and Mrs Taylor's closed bedroom door and stopped. She heard a short laugh and then a slap. Then there was silence. Did they know she was listening? Was it the television? How big was the bedroom? *Did* they have a toilet in there of their own? She heard another quick laugh then a dull thud. She shouldn't be listening. They would know. They would find out. They would add it to their list of suspicions.

Rose continued through the flat and came to the livingroom. It was quiet in there, just the sound of the clock ticking. The boys were going off to the races today. Mr and Mrs Taylor were going to take them. Fay's Fantasy was running. They were going to be given money to bet with and Lance had kept saying he was going to back her both ways to play it safe.

The girls followed their mother into her room. The green shades were drawn and a half-empty fifth of Johnny Walker sat on the bedside table. Wanda dropped onto the bed and fiddled with the virgin bangles around her left wrist. Rose stood in the middle of the room and bit on the nail of her third finger. Her mother turned on the wireless; a sound like a television between channels filled the room. She turned a round knob, her head tilted, her eyebrows narrowed.

Rose took a step towards her. 'Mum?'

'Hang on.' Her mother continued to turn the knob. Snatches of 'Puppy Love', 'Cry Me a River', and 'Do You Know the Way to San Jose?' blurted out in succession. Then someone with an American accent declared 'Butter tastes better.'

'Mum, I —'

'Here it is!' announced her mother, standing up straight. The nasal twang of an announcer came on: 'Yeah, it's a scorcher here at Warwick Farm today. Lucy's Fortune and Captain Cook have been scratched from the fifth. Impulsive is scratched from the sixth. And No Man's Land is gone from the eighth.'

'Good.' Her mother turned it down a little and sat next to Wanda. 'Jackie said Lucy's Fortune could fry Fay's Fantasy.'

'What?' Wanda crossed her legs.

'Fay —' her mother reached for the bottle '— she's got a better chance now.'

'Has,' said Rose.

'What?'

'She has a better chance now.'

'That's right Rosie, she has.'

Her mother poured a nip into a souvenir plastic mug from Tasmania and took a sip. She looked even skinnier, sitting there in her pale blue cotton dress and apron, clutching the mug like a kid on the *Romper Room* show.

Rose crossed her arms. 'Mum, did you have a bet?'

Her mother shook her head. 'Can't afford to.'

'Not even both ways?'

'Not even any way.'

Rose uncrossed her arms and slid her hands into her dress pockets. 'Mum, do you know —'

'Shut up, Rose,' said Wanda. 'The race is just gunna start.'

Her mother took another sip. 'Come and sit over here, luv.' She patted a spot next to her on the bed. Her head swayed slightly. Strands of loose hair had fallen away from the schoolteacher's bun. Inside the room it was hot and humid. The radio crackled and the nasal voice whined on.

Rose shook her head. She walked across to the door, opened it, and slipped away.

The thump of the jukebox pressed up through the floorboards. Someone shrieked and a glass shattered, then there was laughter. A door slammed. The music grew louder. Rose was stretched out on her bed, avoiding it all. Half an hour earlier the boys had burst through the front door, waving five and ten dollar bills in the air like miniature flags at an Anzac day parade. Mr Taylor had barrelled straight into the pub crying, 'My shout! It's my shout!' Mrs Taylor had arrived with an empty champagne glass and left it at the bottom of the stairs before following her husband into the lounge.

Rose rolled onto her side and looked at Wanda, who was standing in front of the open wardrobe.

'You're not gunna get changed again, are you?'

Wanda pulled out a checkered smock top. 'So what if I am?'

Rose lifted her head and thumped it back on the pillow. 'Want to go for a walk before it gets dark? To the shop?'

'No.'

She drew her legs up and slipped her hands between her thighs. 'To the horses?'

Wanda peeled off her T-shirt. 'No.'

She pulled on the smock top and began doing up the buttons. She then sat down on her bed and began brushing her hair. Rose rubbed her eyes and sat up. There was a knock at the door. Rose looked across at her sister.

Wanda swept back her hair. 'You get it, Rose.'

Rose nodded. She pulled the door ajar to find Lucky standing there with a red crepe-paper streamer still looped around his neck. His blond hair was all messed up and he had a dried chocolate ice cream ring around his mouth.

'Want to come down and watch telly?'

Immediately suspicious, Rose peered through the crack in the doorway. His blue eyes widened and looked away. She opened the door a little wider. 'What's on?'

Lucky shrugged. 'I dunno. The usual. *Lost In Space*, I think.'

Rose turned to glance at Wanda, who looked up from her hand mirror and nodded. Rose looked back at Lucky. 'We'll be down in a sec.'

The Brady Bunch theme song babbled into Lucky and Leon's

bedroom. Dark heads of hair appeared in squares on one side of the screen while blonde ones grinned and looked around.

Rose and Wanda stopped in the doorway. The boys had pushed two single beds together and the three of them lounged back on pillows.

Wanda plopped down next to Lance. Rose edged onto a corner of the bed at the foot.

'Move!' cried Lucky. 'Can't see.'

Rose turned. The four of them were lined up next to each other as if posing for a family portrait: first Wanda, then Lance, then Lucky, then Leon.

Leon slid over and made room for her. She lay back on a pillow next to him and fixed her eyes on the black and white portable.

Their bent knees touched. Lance murmured, 'That Cindy's a real dag.' Lucky suddenly crawled off the bed and turned up the volume, then sat on the edge of the bed next to Rose and nudged her over. She was now sandwiched between Leon on her right and Lucky on her left while on the TV the Bradys milled over breakfast.

'We could be the Brady Bunch, you know,' remarked Lucky. 'We could pretend.'

'Whaddya mean?' said Leon.

Lucky leaned closer to Rose, his red streamers touching her arm. 'Well, think about it. Three boys in the Brady Bunch. Lance is as old as Greg. Wanda's as old as Marsha. I'm Peter's age. And you're the same age as Bobby.'

Rose pushed the streamers away. 'What about me?'

'Well,' replied Lucky, 'you're not as old as Jan, but you're older than Cindy, so you'll have to, you know, double up. Pretend you're Cindy *and* Jan.'

'And we come from different families,' said Lance, sitting up.

'We even got a maid like they do,' added Leon.

Rose sat up and glared at him. 'You've got a maid. She's our mother.' Her cheeks were reddening. 'And she's, she's not a maid. She's a housekeeper.'

Leon pinched her arm. 'She's a maid.'

'She *is* a maid,' said Lance. 'She's a servant.'

Lucky squeezed Rose's wrist. 'She's a slave.'

Rose jerked her arm back, but Lucky wouldn't let go. 'Come on little sister Cindy,' he continued. 'Let's play the Brady Bunch.'

'Yeah!' cried Lance, springing onto his knees.

'She's not a slave.'

'She is,' persisted Lucky. 'And you're the slave's daughter. Which do you want to be? Cindy Brady or the slave daughter? Which one?' Lucky tightened his grip and leaned across her. 'Well? Do you want to play or not?'

Rose glanced at Wanda for help, but Wanda continued to gaze at the TV screen, oblivious.

Lucky drove his free hand into his shorts' pocket and pulled out a handful of bills. 'Cause we've won enough money for a slave *and* a slave's daughter, see?'

Rose inched back closer to Leon, but Leon then waved a two-dollar bill so close to her face she could smell it.

'Well, slave daughter? What about it?' Lucky crouched beside Rose and rested his arm on her knee. 'Did you ever see the episode where Peter Brady tickles his sister's fanny?'

'Leave her alone,' said Wanda not taking her eyes off the screen.

'*Did* you?' he added.

'N-no.'

'Or the time Greg roots Marsha?' said Lance, suddenly rolling on top of Wanda.

Wanda shrieked and the two began to scuffle while Lucky pulled at the hem of Rose's dress. One hand pinned her to the bed while the other sprinkled money across her chest. Wanda hurled Lance onto the floor and he pulled her down with him. Rose could feel Lucky's hand on the inside of her thigh. Leon sat in the crack of the two beds like a referee. Lucky's hand moved closer. A grin slipped across his face. 'Cindy or slave?' he whispered.

Rose tightened her lips and spat at him. She pulled up her legs and shoved him, her foot ramming against his stomach.

Lucky fell backwards, the streamers snaking through the air with him. Rose sprung to her feet and the money fell around her like leaves.

Wanda was on her feet also, and the two sisters fled out the door.

'Slave daughter!' cried Lucky, as they ran up the hallway. 'That's all you'll ever be! And if you don't watch it, we'll end up selling you for what we can get!'

Wanda strode up the stairs two at a time. Rose followed, taking them one by one. When she reached the top Wanda had already slammed the bedroom door. Her hand went for the doorknob, but hesitated. Her outstretched hand was shaking like her mother's often did early in the morning.

Rose abruptly turned and paced down the hallway, past the Ladies', past the Gents', past every wooden door with a number. She stopped at the end, at the broom closet, and turned.

She walked back along the hall, each step a little faster. Hands clenched, she ran down the steps, and continued along the downstairs hall, through the Taylor's flat, and into their livingroom. She could still hear the television humming away in the next room.

Rose walked past the gaze of the painted Mrs Taylor and came to the glass doors. It was almost dusk. She was sweating. She wanted to get out.

She opened the door and walked onto the verandah. She wandered down the path, looking around. The rose bush was dying. The sunflowers were closing in on themselves.

Samson trotted up to Delilah, his tongue hanging out, panting. Rose backed away, stepped further down the path. She watched Samson spring up. Her heart thumped. She took tiny, shallow breaths. Delilah pulled away. But Samson whined, galloped forward and leapt up once more, his front legs leaning on Delilah's back. On his hind legs he was as tall as a man. Delilah stood still and hung her head. The pool reflected their animal dance, the way their bodies met, a reflection disturbed only by a dead leaf sailing through the outline of Delilah's back.

Rose swallowed. Lucky's voice was racing through her head, the inflections, the twists. She could still feel his hand on her leg, could still smell the scent of money. Samson shifted closer into Delilah. Cleopatra suddenly barked. Rose edged her way closer to the pen. Her hand touched the wire fence, the gate. Her fingers fumbled with the latch. She held her breath.

Cleopatra lunged through the gateway and in a moment the three dogs were at each other. Cries, yelps and guttural sounds meshed with the attack of teeth against flesh, jaws around a throat, a body hitting the ground. Dust was kicked up as the three dipped and rose. A howl, two dogs locked together, a third plunging in with an open mouth.

Suddenly, the yard was full of people. Mr Taylor was running down the path, yelling. There was a barrage of noise: Mrs Taylor, her mother, Wanda. Rose stood still, her hand clutching the latch of the open gate. Mr Taylor grabbed a collar. Jackie dragged Cleopatra off to the stables. Delilah stood on the pebbled edge around the pool and whimpered. Rose watched Mr Taylor lumber towards her. She could see his yellow teeth, and the black lines of decay between them. He grabbed the collar of her dress and shook her.

Her body went limp. She said nothing; she let him curse, let him jerk her back and forth.

Her mother raised her voice, started arguing with him. She stamped her foot against the ground, untied her apron, scrunched it up in a ball and threw it in Mr Taylor's face. Samson began to howl. The boys ran out into the yard towards Delilah. Rose hung onto the gate to steady herself. Her ears rang. She felt dizzy. The noise circled her head.

'Why?' Mr Taylor bellowed at her. His face was like a big red balloon about to burst.

In her mind the big black film cameras clicked on again. She drew in a deep breath and said, very slowly, 'I didn't do a thing. It was, nothing. I didn't do nothing. I did nothing at all.' And she gazed back at Delilah flanked by the bowed figures of the three boys, and at once felt very big, and very small.

4

THE VISIT

No phone call. No letter. He just turned up at the door one cold afternoon in June, grinning, like he'd only been gone half an hour, had only been down the road to buy a packet of smokes or to sink a few at the local. Rose stood on the straw mat and tugged on his flannelette shirt. Her mother hugged him and started bawling. He looked older. He was wearing glasses thick as Coća-Cola bottles. His blond hair was long, was lapping around his shoulders. He looked like a hippie or something. He had a boxful of bottled beer in his arms. He was going to take a lot of explaining once Mr Cecil got home.

Of course she was glad to see him. He swung her up into the air and she kissed him on the nose three times. She held his hand as her mother led him into the spacious livingroom and sat him in Mr Cecil's brown leather swivel chair.

Mr Cecil was an architect. He had designed this house and had it built into the side of a hill. One wall of the livingroom was just glass and overlooked the grey cluster of Sydney, of buildings pressing into clouds like big knitting needles and a dot of an aeroplane inscribing a smokey white S against the sky.

He put his feet up on the coffee table. He tapped out a rhythm on the arms of the chair. He pulled out a squashed packet of Craven A's and lit one up. Rose sank onto the poof next to him and rested her chin in her hands. She took one of her plaits and slowly began to wrap it around her index finger. What was Mr Cecil going to think?

'Got any jazz?' he asked, as her mother handed him a glass of beer.

Rose stood up. 'There's Cat Stevens.'

'That isn't jazz.'

'I know.' Rose looked down at her brown hushpuppies. 'They're pretty songs, but. The words, you know. The words are nice.'

He pursed his lips. 'No jazz, huh?'

Rose shook her head.

He shrugged. 'All right. Put on Nat Stevens, then.'

'Cat.'

'What?'

'Cat Stevens.'

'Yeah, yeah. All right put him on. Let's hear some sounds.'

After the needle had dropped onto the record player, after the sound of a slow guitar had wandered into the room, Rose looked up to see them, the two girls, the two plump, oversized walking talking ballerina dolls that had made life so miserable. They were Mr Cecil's kids.

Trixie, the older one, had her hair braided and pinned in a spiral around her head. She was wearing a string of pearls and a ruby ring she got out of a machine for twenty cents. The younger one had pigtails with a red and white polka-dotted ribbon and a faded pink tutu that was too big. Her real name was Denise, but everyone called her Dixie, because it rhymed with Trixie. Dixie and Trixie. Trixie and Dixie. They were going to grow up and be famous singers, a sister act. They already knew 'The Impossible Dream' and half of 'Chitty Chitty Bang Bang'. They could hum the theme song to *Hawaii Five O* and do the twist. Rose couldn't do any of these things. They were bonkers. They were up the creek. They were too fat to become famous.

They stopped in the doorway and stared at him. He was dragging on his Craven A, blowing smoke rings towards the ceiling. Rose felt a sinking feeling inside, like a half-baked cake slowly dropping into itself. He shouldn't have come. He should have stayed away. He should have written a letter. He should have rung instead.

'Hello,' said her mother, putting down her glass of beer. She walked towards them, wiping her palm against her skirt.

Trixie fiddled with her ring and Dixie sneezed. Rose drummed the heel of her shoe against the polished wood floor. He didn't take his feet off the coffee table.

'Girls,' continued her mother, 'this is my —' she glanced at him, at a smoke ring wafting towards the window '— this is my brother. From Queensland. He just got down from Queensland. He's just come down to visit.' Her mother took a step forward. 'Say hello, girls.'

The sisters eyed him. 'Hello.'

'His name is, is Eddie. You can call him Uncle Eddie.'

Rose swallowed as her mother shot her a glance.

'Uncle Eddie's from Queensland.'

'You already said that,' said Trixie.

'Yeah,' added Dixie.

'That's right.' Her mother gave a quick laugh and walked back to her beer. 'So I did.'

He inclined forward and butted out his cigarette. Rose sat at his feet and rested her head on his knee. Trixie and Dixie watched him from the black leather couch on the other side of the coffee table. Her mother sat in the rocking chair, not rocking, but sitting still and nursing her beer.

Rose touched the side of his worn and faded gymboots. They were strung with yellow football laces and tied in a double bow. 'Where've you been?' she said, not looking up.

'He's been to Queensland, silly,' said Trixie. 'Your mum just told us a million times.'

Rose ignored her. She pulled at the yellow laces. 'I wrote to you, you know. I wrote you two letters but you never wrote any back.'

Trixie clenched her fists. 'How could you, how could you write him a letter if you didn't even know where he lived?'

'I did, but —'

'Well?'

'But I —'

He leaned forward. 'I move around a lot, see? I'm always on the move. Always travelling. Always on the go. That's me.'

He picked up his beer and drank the rest of it down without pausing for a breath.

Rose wished that Trixie would shut up. She wished that Trixie would open her mouth and that her jaw would suddenly lock, and that she'd walk about for the rest of her life looking like one of those clowns that rotate their heads from side to side and get to have a few ping-pong balls dropped down their throats on the odd lucky occasion.

'Going up to Darwin next week,' he said, staring into his empty glass.

Rose felt the sinking sensation once more. He was going to leave again. He was going to go. And everything would be the same, just like yesterday, and the day before.

'*Darwin?*' echoed her mother. 'Why on earth would you want to —'

'A change,' he said. 'I feel like a change. You know? Got to get my head together. Turn over a new leaf — you know — all that crap.'

He set his glass on the table and ruffled Rose's hair.

Dixie kicked off her sandshoes. 'Are you a swaggy?'

'A swagman?' He refilled his glass. 'Nope. Not me.' He burped and put down the bottle. 'But my brother Jack is.'

Trixie turned to Rose's mother. 'How many brothers do you *have?*'

Rose smiled. 'Three and a half.'

Trixie frowned at her. 'What are you talking about?'

'Uncle Eddie's the half.'

Her mother laughed and clinked her glass against his.

'Well, what *are* you then?' demanded Trixie, doubling the pearls around her neck.

'He's a salesman,' said Rose's mother.

'He's a gypsy,' said Rose.

Trixie frowned again. He put down his glass. 'I'm a movie star.'

'You are not.'

He leaned back and crossed his legs. 'All right. I'm a garbo.'

'No you aren't.'

He patted his rhythm against the arms of the chair again. 'Well, what do you *want* me to be?'

Trixie jumped up. 'Whatever you are!'

'Well, I am! I am whatever I am. See?' He drummed his index finger against his chest. 'I'm Uncle Eddie.'

Rose stood up and fell into his lap. 'He's Uncle Eddie.'

Her mother stood up and bustled the girls out to the kitchen to find some chocolate biscuits.

Rose hummed along with the record and paused to rub noses with him. 'Ask me where I'm gunna swim to.'

He grinned. 'OK. Where you gunna swim to?'

'I'm gunna swim around Australia. I'm gunna follow you.' She paused and glanced into the kitchen. Her mother's head hovered above the open fridge door. Rose lowered her voice. 'Do you know about Mr Cecil? Larry?'

'Your mother's boss.'

Rose glanced into the kitchen again and nodded. 'Do you know that Mum sometimes —' She fidgeted with a button on his flannelette shirt. Her mother closed the fridge door and walked back into the livingroom.

'Want a bicky, Rose?'

'No.' Rose looked at his thick glasses and tapped him on the shoulder. She tightened her lips and kissed at the air, her lips making a squeaky, smacking sound.

'What's that for?' said her mother, sitting down on the couch opposite.

Rose turned. 'It means, it means I want a sip of beer.'

'Funny way of asking for it.'

He reached for his glass. 'She's a funny kid.'

'You're a funny uncle.'

She rested her head on his shoulder and gazed out through the plate-glass wall. An aeroplane hung above the towering cylinder of Australia Square. Outside, beyond the city, was a whole world he was going to disappear into while she and her mother would be stuck in the house inside the hill with the two dancing bears who talked too much.

'What's it like?' he asked.

Her mother looked up from her beer. 'What?'

'Living here.'

'It's —' her mother took a sip '— it's a job. Better than the last one. Pay's better. You know, less work.'

Trixie and Dixie were still in the kitchen, measuring out Milo into plastic mugs. Dixie spilled some milk onto the brown ceramic tiles.

He held up his glass. Rose took a sip and made a face. It was bubbly and bitter, a sour soft drink.

'Where's Wanda?' he said suddenly.

Her mother looked down at the floor. 'Living with Mag. I could only bring one of them, you know, so I —'

'How's Mag going?'

'Fine. Pregnant again. She's OK.' Her mother looked up. 'Wanda's a bit upset — you know — having to go off and live with Mag and everything.' She reached for her cigarettes. 'Ned's still up on the farm with Bob.'

He gulped down the rest of his beer and placed the glass on the table. He looked at her mother. 'I missed you.'

Her mother lit up a Viscount. 'I missed you.'

Rose touched his hand. 'Why did it take so long?'

He pulled his hand away and scratched his head. He looked at her mother. 'Let's crack another one.'

Her mother went to the fridge and pulled out another bottle. Dixie and Trixie followed her back in. More beer was poured and he licked the side of his glass where the froth was overflowing.

Dixie swept away a sprinkle of Milo powder from her tutu. She sat down in the rocking chair and looked across at him. 'Are you an alcoholic?'

He looked up and cleared his throat. 'No. Why would you —?'

'Are you, are you older or younger than her?' Dixie nodded to Rose's mother.

He sipped his beer. 'Older.'

'Why do you grow your hair so long?'

'Keeps my ears warm.'

'Our mother, our mother doesn't have any brothers. Or sisters. Our mother is an only, an only child.'

'Their mother,' said Rose, turning to face him, 'ran away on a P&O cruise around the world with another bloke.'

'Rose!' Her mother slid to the edge of the couch.

'Well it's true!'

'Rose, just be quiet, will you?'

'Our mother loves us,' said Trixie, wiping her mouth with the back of her hand. 'She sent us grass skirts from Fiji and a shell necklace.'

'It's plastic,' said Rose.

'It is not. It's shell. Real shell. She sent it to us airmail. With a postcard. A postcard from, from Fiji with a picture on the front of a, of a hula dancer.'

'You wanna see me dance,' he said, sliding Rose off his knee. He pushed himself up out of the chair and suddenly began patting out a rhythm against the wood floor with his feet. Head bent, hands clenched, he grinned and shuffled along to 'Tea for the Tillerman'. He drummed out soft staccato beats that fell into each other and multiplied into a train rhythm. Rose followed him around the chair, watching his feet. She'd never seen him do it before. He was a genius. He'd leave Shirley Temple for dead.

He finished with his arms planing out in a diagonal and one leg cocked up in the air at the back.

The girls clapped while Rose's mother poured brandy into balloon glasses. Rose gazed out the window. The sun was beginning to sink, shadowing the city with fire colour. Mr Cecil. It wouldn't be long now. He'd arrive with his briefcase and look over the pair of glasses always perched at the tip of his nose.

'We can dance,' announced Trixie.

'And sing,' added Dixie.

Before Rose could protest they were up out of their seats, running into their bedroom to put on their costumes.

'They're awful,' said Rose.

He dropped onto the couch with her mother. His hand touched her knee and for a moment Rose felt a change. New hope.

She walked towards the couch and sat down beside him. She rested her hand upon the hand that lay upon her mother's knee. She looked up at his glasses. 'You don't really want to go to, to Darwin, do you?'

He pulled his hand away. 'Course I do.'

The record player clicked off. A blanket of darkness was falling across the city. Rose gritted her teeth. Take us away. To Queensland. To Darwin. To the sun.

He and her mother sipped brandy and chased it with beer. He suddenly laughed and pinched Rose's nose. 'Remember the time we took you to that pub on the water? With the jazz? And you got up and played a drum solo while the musos were taking a break? In your pyjamas, your dressing gown and slippers. Brought the house down. Remember that?'

Rose nodded. 'At the Seabreeze. You bought me pink lemonade. We lived with you then.'

He guzzled his beer again and looked out the window. 'Isn't it time for your tea?'

'No. We're waiting for Mr Cecil. Mr Cecil eats tea with us every night. Then he smokes two cigarettes and reads the paper. Then drinks a glass, a glass of brandy and has a bath.' Rose stood up and walked around the coffee table. 'Then he comes out in his dressing gown. And slippers. And he sits in his chair.' Rose dropped onto the brown leather. 'And, and watches *Pick-a-box*. Then *Homicide*. Then —' she paused and swung her legs back and forth '— then *Perry Mason* and, and, what's it called? *Laugh In*. Then he watches *Laugh In*. And then Mum gives him another brandy and she has one, too. And then he turns the telly off and they —'

'Rose?'

'Yes?' Rose looked across at her mother nestled in the crook of his arm.

'Could you go and wash the spuds for tea?'

Rose shrugged and slid off the chair. 'I don't even like spuds.'

She wandered into the kitchen and fished out four potatoes from a sack hanging by the fridge. After filling up the sink, she submerged them in water and rubbed the dirt away. She didn't even like spuds. She didn't like Mr Cecil. She didn't even like Cat Stevens that much. But that's all there was. She pulled the plug and put the potatoes on the dishrack to dry.

Rose found them gone when she walked back into the livingroom. Dixie and Trixie were slumped on the couch, decked out in grass skirts and beads, lipstick and rouge. Trixie still wore her pearls and ruby ring.

'Where'd they go?'

Trixie pointed to the bedroom that Rose and her mother shared. The door was closed. 'Your Mum wanted to show him the family photo album. Don't know why, but. Youse don't have a family.'

'Neither do youse.'

Trixie stood up. 'We do so. We've got photos to prove it.'

'Well you can cut your mum out of all the pictures.'

'Our mother loves us. See?' Trixie turned in a circle. She swung her hips from side to side and made a scooping motion with her hands.

'She never forgot us,' said Dixie, her grass skirt rustling as she stood and imitated her sister. 'She sends us presents. Your uncle never even sent you a postcard from Queensland. He don't love you. Our mother loves us. She sends us things. Lots of things. Her boyfriend's rich.'

Rose backed onto the couch. 'He does so love me. He's, he's here, isn't he? He came to see me, didn't he? He's not, he didn't go away and leave me like your mother did.'

A sound came from the bedroom. Her mother's voice. Like she'd just unwrapped a gift.

Trixie suddenly stopped dancing and rested her hands on her hips. 'He's only your uncle. Uncles and aunts never love you as much as your mother and father. Lots of times they even hate you.'

Rose sunk further into the couch.

Trixie pointed her toe and lifted into a pirouette. 'Our mother's gunna go to Egypt and Spain.'

Dixie sunk into a plié. 'Japan and America.'

'China and Hong Kong.' Trixie began waltzing around the room with an imaginary partner. 'She'll send home kimonos and sombreros and an Elvis Presley T-shirt. A Mexican hat. Wooden clogs. And a, a skirt. A kilt. A red kilt with some bagpipes and a little black hat. A beret.'

Rose heard another sound. It was him. It sounded as if he had a belly ache.

Dixie leapt up into the air and sailed towards the television. 'And when she gets to England she's gunna send for us.' Dixie trotted around in a circle, flapping her arms. 'And you and your mum will have to go because our dad can look after himself, see?'

'What?' said Rose, sliding to the edge of the couch.

Dixie smiled. 'You'll have to go. Soon. Pretty soon. She should be in England by next month.'

Trixie danced by the couch. 'Next week.'

Dixie hopped from one foot to the other. 'Maybe tomorrow.'

Rose curled her plait around her finger again. They couldn't even lie well. Their mother would never send for them. Their mother would never come home. She'll sail around the world for the rest of her life. And her mother will serve brandy to Mr Cecil every night. And they'll all be stuck together, inside the house inside the hill, watching the world from a box seat, through the huge window, the glass screen.

A cry came from the bedroom. And then another. And another.

'What are they *doing* in there?' Trixie frowned and gazed at the bedroom door.

Dixie sat in the rocking chair. 'Sounds like she's having a nightmare.'

'She's not sleeping, silly. She couldn't be asleep.'

'She's sick,' said Rose.

'All that grog,' said Trixie.

Dixie rocked back and forth. '*He* must be sick, too, then.'

They waited for what seemed like ages, but he and her mother didn't come out. They turned on the television and watched *Gomer Pyle*. They ate the rest of the chocolate biscuits. They glanced at the bedroom door during the commercials.

Trixie told her to go in and see what had happened to them. They might be dead. All that booze. It might have killed them. But Rose wanted to wait. She wanted to wait before she opened the door.

They waited some more. They watched *Get Smart*. They drank some more Milo. They didn't glance at the door so often.

Dixie changed the channel. Trixie tried to smoke a Craven A. Rose picked up his gymboots. He'd left them under the couch. She slipped them on and tightened the laces.

She stood up and tried to dance as he had. Trixie coughed and tried to blow a smoke ring as he had. Dixie put her feet up on the table.

Suddenly, the front door slammed. Rose jumped. Trixie coughed and spluttered and ground the cigarette into the ashtray. Dixie slid her feet off the table.

'What's going on?' Mr Cecil stood in the kitchen doorway and observed the room. Rose looked at him. Then she looked at the empty beer bottles, the brandy decanter on the table, a record on the floor, the grass skirts on Trixie and Dixie.

'Bloody potatoes in the dishrack.' He put down his briefcase. 'What's going on?'

'Nancy's brother,' said Trixie.

'What?' He walked towards them.

'It's my uncle,' said Rose, twisting her braid again.

'He's just come to visit. Just a bit. Just a while.'

Mr Cecil frowned.

'Where's Nancy?'

Rose hesitated. She bit her lip.

'Well?'

Rose looked down at the big gymboots. There'd be years in front of the glass window, years of 'The Impossible Dream' and 'Swan Lake'. Years of brandy before bed. And he'd be off in Darwin, sunbaking.

She took Mr Cecil by the hand and led him to the bedroom. Her feet were swimming inside the gymboots. She turned the knob and opened the door. Mr Cecil hung back. Mr Cecil was polite. Rose walked in first.

A bedside lamp glowed in the darkness. She found her mother asleep, a sheet coiled around her body, flanking one breast and gathered beneath her chin. He was twisted up in it, too, limbs caught in a frozen dance, an arm slung across her mother's waist.

Rose smiled. She walked back outside and looked up at Mr Cecil. It would be loud. It would be nasty. It would be over quickly. She took his hand. She nodded. She led him into the bedroom's green half-light.

5

HAPPY HOUR

It wasn't living in a basement that was the problem. And it wasn't that they were all back together, squeezed into two rooms. It wasn't so bad sleeping on the floor. And it was fun having tomatoes for tea. She didn't mind the cockroaches, or taking turns sitting at the table. The real problem was that her father never stopped practising, and he hadn't had a gig in years.

He'd hocked his wedding ring and paid the balance on an old upright Baldwin. He'd parked it in front of the only window in the basement. All day, she'd watch him play Monk's more difficult compositions, like 'Off Minor', or Parker's 'Donna Lee', then 'A Night in Tunisia', followed by a sequence of other Dizzy Gillespie numbers. He'd play every melody he knew with both hands in every key. He'd play them fast. He'd play them slow. He'd reharmonise them. He'd make them sound better. He was brilliant. He should be on telly. He was going to be famous.

But it drove everyone else up the wall. Her mother and Wanda went to visit Granny all the time. Ned stayed over at his friend's place. No one came home 'til after dark. And Rose wondered whether it was just out of a need for money that her mother called up an old boss one day and finally got him a gig down on Castlereagh Street. Rose knew her mother had to get him out of the house for a little while, just for a few hours a day.

The day of the big gig, everyone, as usual, cleared out. Only Rose stayed behind to listen. He was up at seven, lifting Nicolas Slonimsky's *Thesaurus of Scales and Melodic Patterns* to the wooden lip above the keys, not even stopping for a cup of tea. He started at the beginning of the book and only paused between each scale to announce its name to her.

By three or so she was standing on her head in a corner of the room, as he had taught her, while he clowned around in front of the fireplace in a black suit sizes too big for him. He was dancing to an Oscar Peterson record. The waistline of his trousers slipped over his hips and the bell-bottom hems kept getting caught under his feet.

'Dad?' Rose found herself looking at an upside-down pair of thongs flapping against his heels. 'Are you really gunna wear that?'

She saw his feet dance towards her.

'Well, they said I had to wear a dinner suit, and this is the only one I've got. Maybe we can use some safety pins or something.' He paused and hitched up his trousers. 'Do you know where my bow tie is?'

Rose pushed off from the wall. Her legs arced through the air. Her feet landed on the floor with a thud. 'Last time I saw it, you let me wear it to school for our end of year party.'

Her father sighed. 'It could be anywhere.'

'No, it's somewhere,' she said, standing up.

He slid his hands into his pockets. 'Makes you feel more relaxed doesn't it?'

Rose touched his arm to steady herself. 'Yes, Dad, I feel real relaxed.'

'It's all that blood,' he continued. 'All that blood circulating through your head, you know? Very good for the brain. Good for the head. Good for the constitution.'

Rose felt a little dizzy and ambled across to the bed. He stood still, hands in pockets, staring at a spot on the floor. She edged closer to the pile of sheet music at the end of the bed. 'Are you all right?' she asked, standing up again. 'Dad?'

He looked across at her. 'Do you want to come?'

'Where?'

He drew his hands out of his pockets. 'To the gig.'

Rose walked towards him. 'Can I? Will they let me?'

'Course they will. You're Lenny Partridge's kid, aren't you?' She felt his hand ruffle her hair. 'Anyway, you can get the applause going at the end of each tune. You know, get 'em going a bit. Stir up the crowd. Always helps to have a few mates in the audience. Now come on,' he continued, pinching her on the nose, 'and help me get it together. Let's find that bloody bow tie, eh?'

Together they rummaged through a drawer, pulling out cotton underpants, a few singlets, a broken metronome, and a yellowing photograph of him hunched over a piano with a young Nat King Cole backstage at the Sydney Stadium. On top of the upright piano a balloon glass full of amber liquid glowed above her father's head like a spotlight.

Rose stopped and looked at his baggy trousers. 'You need a belt.'

'What?'

'A belt.' She snatched up a black leather one that was strewn amongst the pile of socks and underwear at his feet.

He stood still and let her thread the belt through the loopholes, his arms planing out to the sides like a nervous bride-to-be at a wedding-gown fitting.

His hand met the end of the belt as it emerged through the last loop and deftly flipped it through the gold buckle. The trousers drew up around his waist in tight folds. She tucked in the tail of the shirt while he smoothed down the frills in front.

'You look gas,' she declared, circling him.

'You reckon?'

'Yep.'

'Need the bow tie though, don't I?'

'I s'pose. Where are your shoes?'

'Under the bed,' he replied. 'Hop down and get 'em, eh? I don't wanna get my pants mucked up.'

She kneeled on the floor, an arm groping around over what felt like an empty beer can, a roll of toilet paper, a small picture frame, and finally produced two black leather shoes coated in dust.

He slipped them on and she rubbed them clean with an odd sock. 'Dad?' she said, suddenly looking up at him. 'How do you play that one thing — um — that one thing in' — she stood up — 'in that song. The one you were just playing before.'

He slid his hands into his pockets. 'Which thing are you talking about?'

'The part where — um — it goes all funny.' She glanced at the piano. 'You know. The part before, before the —'

'The bridge?'

Rose nodded. He guided her across to the piano and they sat down together on the stool.

'See?' he said, his fingers darting between the keys. 'Not that hard. Reckon you can do it?'

Rose swallowed. 'Don't do it so fast.'

He nodded, and gradually the passage slowed down, like a music box unwinding to its last notes. 'Do you want me to write it out for you?'

'Nup,' she replied, her hand straining to fall into the same pattern two octaves higher. Hair unbraided, it fell across her face like a golden curtain falling between the keys and her vision. Suddenly, she felt his hand drop onto hers, pressing each finger into place. The piano coughed out slow and deliberate sounds. His hand felt like a warm glove around hers. She swung back her head, laughing. Her fingers moved beneath his, anticipating each note. He laughed too, and drew his hand away. Rose repeated the phrase without hesitating while he strode down to the lower register in counterpoint.

'Bravo!' he cried when they had finished.

Rose slid off the stool and took a low bow.

'Bravo!' he said again, as she pretended to curtsey with an imaginary skirt. 'I'll make a muso out of you yet. You got a good feel, you know that? A good feel. Can't teach that. You either got a good feel or you haven't. That's what ol' Roddo used to say. Remember him? Roddy Michaels?'

'Yep.' Rose sat back down on the stool. 'Down at Coogee.'

'Yeah, good ol' Roddo. You never heard him play, did you?'

Rose shook her head.

'Man, what a bloody monster! If you think I'm good, you wanna hear Roddo. He doesn't just make the piano talk, you know — anyone can do that — Roddo can make that baby tell its life story!'

Her father smiled to himself and, though he wasn't really playing anything in particular, continued to flirt with the keys, punctuating his sentences with deep, resonant chords.

'He used to teach me, you know. Did you know that?'

Rose nodded.

'Bloody old bugger took me down to the Captain Cook after my first lesson and got me pissed. On port. Ruby Red. Bloody awful stuff. Did I ever tell you about that?'

Rose looked up at him.

'He started writing out music on serviettes,' continued her father, 'and scatting it out loud to the barmaid as he went along. Ended up spending all his dough — plus the money I gave him for my lesson — betting in a bloody two-up game. I said, "Rod, you're too good for this. Why are you wasting your dough in this joint?" And Roddo says, real cool, "She'll be right, Len watch this." And he got up on the bar and started yelling and carrying on. He was trying to auction off his bloody music — can you believe that? He held up the serviette — all scribbled over — and said, "Who'll gimme five bucks for this important contribution to the Australian Arts?"'

Her father started laughing again. Rose laid a hand on the keys, remembering Roddy's wrinkled, sunburnt face, the way he could make his false teeth jump in and out of his mouth in a moment.

'Bloody ol' Rod,' said her father again. 'He's a bloody beauty. Bit of a boozer. But hell, no muso in this town can touch him. Not one. He could cut anyone.

'I remember once — down at Roosevelt's — he was playing with an eighteen-piece band, I think they were playing something like — what was it — "Sing, Sing, Sing". Yeah, that's right, "Sing, Sing, Sing". So ol' Roddo's playing away — and I'm standing just off to the side watching — and when the drummer takes his solo, Roddo stands up, walks off the stage, spews into a trombone case, walks back on and comes back in without missing a beat.' Her father laughed. 'How's that, eh? Didn't miss a beat!'

He shook his head. 'Bloody ol' Rod. He got me my first gig, you know —'

Rose nodded and slid off the stool. 'Dad,' she said, glancing at the clock, 'it's twenty-five after!'

'What?!'

'Time to go.'

'Shit, it's this bloody daylight savings that's throwing me off. It feels like two o'clock or something!'

He hurried to the mirror and ran a comb through his hair. Aqua-coloured opal cufflinks were fastened. A few drops of Brut frilled around his neck.

'Have you seen my wallet?' he asked, nosing around his sheet music. 'It's got the address in it and everything.'

Rose shook her head.

He fell to his knees and rummaged through the pile of under-wear. 'It's got the address in it. I'm gunna — I'm gunna be late.'

She looked on the mantlepiece, the piano, searched the drawers.

'Shit! And I haven't even found the bow tie, *or* the wallet.' He was going through his pockets. He was sweating. His hands were beginning to tremble. 'What am I going to do if I can't find it? Where the hell is it? I know it's here somewhere.' He turned in a circle looking at the floor. 'I know it is. Jesus, what time it is now? We have to get the bus. Where the hell is it? I'm gunna be late.'

Rose swallowed. She watched him turning in a circle. She glanced around the room. An inch-long cockroach crawled up the side of the refrigerator, tracking across a cellotaped black-and-white photograph of Thelonious Monk.

Rose walked across to the wardrobe and pulled out his jacket. She helped him slip it on. Suddenly, he let out a sigh. 'Put your shoes on,' he said, withdrawing from his pocket a split vinyl wallet and a black bow tie.

She trailed behind him as they made their way along Darlinghurst Road. Before leaving the room, at the last moment, she had flung on her white lace Holy Communion dress, complete with pearl buttons, and the pair of red tap shoes that she'd found at the Wayside Chapel Opportunity Shop. Only the right heel tap was still attached and every second step she took was punctuated with a metronomic click.

They passed the pinball parlour and the fruit shop. A middle-aged woman was wearing a pink sequinned bikini while leaning in the doorway of The Love Machine. Her father didn't seem to notice. Rose stared, noticing how tight elastic bit tanned loose skin, how long false eyelashes fanned upwards.

They stepped around a caricature artist and his easel outside Woollies, and a greying one-legged man in dirty jeans strumming on the three strings of his guitar while his crutches formed a line on the ground between him and the people passing by.

They got on a double-decker bus at Kingsgate — Rose insisted that they sit on top at the front — and presently found themselves rumbling down the hill of William Street.

She was glad her mother had found him the job. She imagined him onstage at the Town Hall, at the revolving restaurant on top of Australia Square, at the Opera House, in the Recording Hall, playing a concert Steinway. He deserved it. He was the best. He had jammed with Nat King Cole and got drunk with Count Basie. He once played for two days straight in the Mullumbimbi Pub. Only he had recognised that Shiny Watson was really just imitating Les McCann records and had told him to get fucked.

They stood, hand-in-hand, before two large plate-glass doors on Castlereagh Street. She gazed at her dishevelled hair. He let go of her hand and straightened his tie. He took hold of her wrist. His hand was still shaking.

'Think they'll let me in?' she said, addressing his reflection.

'I'll just sit you in the corner with a soft drink. She'll be apples. No worries.'

He reached out for the thick brass handle and pulled back the door.

Stepping into a veil of smoke and perfume, they picked their way around small round tables, muffled conversations, a pair of legs outstretched on a fat briefcase. The bar was large, windowless and dimly lit, illuminated only by imitation gas lamps that craned out from the walls.

He installed her in the corner closest to the black baby grand and shuffled off to the bar to find the manager.

There was a colour television mounted in the opposite corner. The sound was turned down low, but every now and then Bugs Bunny's whiny 'What's up, Doc?' leaked into the room, and those who sat alone, mooning over middies of beer, looked up in recognition.

She tucked her hair behind her ear and gazed up at her father. He was talking to a man in a tight grey suit; the waistcoat buttons strained to remain in their places and the waistline of his trousers cowered beneath a round pot belly.

Her father was listening and nodding. Then he shook the man's hand, turned, and ordered something from the barmaid.

Rose eyed the keys, the black glow of polished lacquer, and Yamaha written in gold. This is what he deserved. A piano like Liberace's. She imagined TV cameras, a candelabra, her father introducing himself with a big smile: 'Live from the Argyle Club'.

He handed her a glass of Orchy and walked across to the piano with a drink of his own. Instead of arranging his music, he simply swooped it up off the stool and dumped it on the floor. Rose crossed her legs. Her mouth found the paper straw. She watched him sit, place his glass at the edge of the keys, open and close his hands in a quick warm-up.

She glanced at the TV. Foghorn Leghorn was swaggering around a barnyard, his southern drawl stuttering below the hum of tired conversations and the cash register's money tray springing out like an open mouth. Her father lifted his hands. Rose held her breath.

His first sounds were tentative notes of Monk's introduction to "Round Midnight', a mere whisper sneaking into the room. Then his fingers hit the first five notes of the chorus and curled around the higher keys in a flourish. A shiver ran through her body. He played this for her often, like a bedtime story, when she lay wrapped in a blanket on the floor, unable to sleep.

Head bowed, he followed the changes, taking turns, until phrases sank and rose into some new twist he coaxed from the keys. She realised that it was different every time, as if he were reinventing the melody's distant sorrow and beauty. He touched the keys as though they might break under the weight of his hands, then suddenly persuaded tension. He seduced sound into a corner of compliance.

The resonance of his last note was met with a blank silence, only disturbed by the rasp of a man ordering two scotch-on-the-rocks at the bar. Rose stiffened in her chair and blushed. The solitary sound of her clapping seemed strange to her, worse than silence. Slowly, his right arm extended for the glass. He tipped his head back, drank, and replaced the glass, empty.

She saw him draw in a deep breath and sigh, his hands returning to the keyboard as if in sleepwalk. He pressed out the first, slow passage of 'Mood Indigo', nudging fills into space, lingering on the higher notes like shy hands around a woman's waist. But the ballad couldn't penetrate the mumble of drinking that reigned throughout the bar.

Rose cringed when she saw the manager stalking towards them.

'What,' he demanded, frowning over the keys, 'do you think you're doing?'

Her father stopped playing suddenly and looked up. 'Whatsa matter?'

The manager hitched up his trousers and rested his hands on his hips. Rose slid to the edge of her chair.

'This is *happy hour*, mate!'

'So?'

'So can't you play anything a bit more...happy?'

Her father didn't answer.

'Now, now don't get me wrong,' stammered the manager, 'you play real pretty and everything, but this isn't a funeral, you know. Can't you play something a bit more, you know, *lively*? To sell drinks? Something they can hum along with?'

Her father stared at the keys. 'What would you suggest?'

The manager frowned again and scratched his neck. 'I dunno, mate. I'm not much of a —' He fiddled with his gold ring. 'Do you know, um, what's it called? It used to be a real biggy, um —' He slid his hands into his pockets. Expressionless, her father didn't move.

'Hounddog!' exclaimed the manager. '"You Ain't Nothin' but a Hounddog." You know that?'

'No.'

'You sure? It used to be a —'

'Never heard of it.'

On the TV screen, the coyote was falling off a cliff, while the barmaid served cold baby frankfurts and jatz at the tables.

'Well, I dunno,' whined the manager. 'Just play something, you know, something *happy*.'

Her father glanced at him, nodded, and leant down to pick up his pile of sheet music. The manager ran a hand across his balding head and turned. Rose slurped down the dregs of her orange juice, looking away.

She waited for a moment when she could make him smile, connect with him, could pull a face and make him laugh. But he wouldn't cast an eye towards her and instead raised a finger to the barmaid and propped up a dogeared chart in front of him.

Rose was dismayed to hear 'Beer Barrel Polka' come thundering out of the piano in straight, up-tempo $\frac{2}{2}$, just like her great aunt's babbling pianola. She'd never heard him play that way. It was corny. It was stilted. It was rinky-dink.

Beers were put down and heads looked up. The manager grinned, half a frankfurt protruding from his mouth, and began to clap off the beat. The barmaid lifted her arms and shook her breasts momentarily in a mock belly dance.

Her father hammered the keys while staring deadpan at the chart. It sounded like an accompaniment to a silent film. Rose blushed again. She wanted him to stop. He was speeding up, speeding up as if in a race. Notes ran together. It was a clumsy splutter. His eyes dropped from the chart to the keyboard. His hands fell anywhere, in rapid succession, deviating from the melody in a tantrum of noise.

'Listen, mate.' It was the manager again. He was tapping her father on the shoulder. But her father didn't acknowledge him, couldn't stop slapping the keys at random. Chunks of discordant sound filled the bar. People covered their mouths and whispered.

'Hey, mate!' Another tap on the shoulder. Still no response. Rose gripped the side of her chair, saw the way his two index fingers suddenly stiffened and dropped onto the keyboard to peck out a slow, deliberate 'Chopsticks'. Hunched over, he continued to repeat it at a maddeningly slow tempo and even managed to make a few mistakes.

'*Hey you!*' The manager grabbed him by the shoulder and wrenched him back. Rose sprang onto her feet, hands clenched.

'OK,' snarled the manager. 'We've had *enough*. Here's your fifty bucks. Now *piss off*. And if you ever show up here again, I'll shove that piano right up your *arse.*'

Her father stood up, straightened his jacket, and offered a slight half bow to the man. He took the outstretched bills, folded them, and slipped them into his back pocket. He smoothed back his hair, picked up his pile of music and nodded to Rose.

They made their way past silent stares towards the door. Rose was hurrying, wanting to get out of the place, but her father stopped abruptly at the end of the bar and turned.

'Give us a bottle of plonk, luv?' he said to the barmaid, who was eyeing him uneasily. 'Ruby Red. A flagon, eh?'

The barmaid hesitated, and then disappeared into an adjoining room. He slapped ten dollars onto the bar. Rose held onto the hem of his jacket and cast sidelong looks at the crowd. The barmaid returned, frowning, hugging a flagon of burgundy-coloured port in her arms.

A fading daylight fell upon them as they stepped out into the street. He held his sheet music with one hand and the flagon of port with the other. Rose still clutched the hem of his jacket.

They both paused on the street, confused about which way to go. Cars crawled along in lanes, edging their way back to the suburbs. A man to their left in a tattered brown coat was gazing into a garbage bin as if it were a wishing well. Her father drew in a deep breath and suddenly started laughing.

'Hey,' he said. 'How about we go round and see ol' Roddo?'

Rose looked up at him.

'We could have a jam,' he continued. 'We could show him how good you play, eh?'

Rose bit her lip and shook her head.

'But I thought you wanted to see him again. And hear him play —'

'Let's go home, Dad.'

'We could get some lemonade for you. Have a little party. You can play "Willow Weep for Me". We'll get some chips, too.'

She reached up and took his arm. 'No, Dad.'

'We could get a cab over. Got plenty of dough. Wait 'til you hear old Roddo play. He doesn't just make that piano talk —'

'Come on, Dad.'

'He can cut anyone.'

Rose glanced at the man to her left as he pulled a half-eaten sandwich out of the bin. 'I know,' she said.

Her father hugged the flagon closer to his chest, sighed, and cleared his throat. There was an awkward silence as he looked past the frills on his shirt and studied his baggy trousers. She ran a hand across her white lace dress. A dribble of orange juice graced the folds at her waist and her feet felt cramped inside the red shoes. They were both looking down when a horn on the harbour blew and a yellow cab rattled by.

'Come on,' she said, tightening her grip on his arm. 'Let's go, Dad. Let's go home.'

6

THE VELVET ROOSTER

'Well, what do *you* think?' said Rose, as she lowered the nail polish brush to her sister's thumb.

'I think he's too young for her,' replied Wanda.

'I think he talks funny.'

'I think Mum could do better.'

She dragged thick, red nail polish across her sister's thumb and lowered the brush back into the bottle.

'When he took me out yesterday,' said Rose, 'he bought me a dress. He took me to a restaurant and bought me a prawn cocktail and a piece of pavlova.'

'You've already told me fifty thousand times. Anyway, that's nothing.' Wanda held out her index finger. 'He's just buttering you up. Wait a while. We'll see.'

'I liked Norman better,' said Rose.

'I liked Stan better,' said Wanda.

'I liked Ian, no, *Whoopsie*. Whoopsie was the best.'

'Whoopsie had a crooked nose,' said Wanda, softly blowing on her nails. 'He was fat, too. Stan was the best.'

Rose drew the brush out of the bottle again and let it linger on the rim as excess polish ran off.

'What do you think his real name is?' said Wanda.

'It's not George.'

'No, it's not George,' agreed Wanda.

'I think he said it was, um —' Rose frowned momentarily, drawing tiny, invisible circles in the air with the brush. 'Mo, Mo —'

'*Mo?*'

'No, not Mo. Mo, Mohammed.'

'Mohammed?'

'Yes. Mohammed.'

'I like George better.'

'I liked Whoopsie better.'

'Whoopsie's in gaol, Rose.'

'I know, I know.' Rose lowered the brush to her sister's third finger. 'We'll just have to settle for George.'

The two sisters tiptoed to the doorway of their bedroom and peeped around. He was clumping down the hallway with a red plastic string bag full of scrunched-up clothes. He also carried a plaster statue of a woman whose bare breasts pointed above the grip of his hand.

The girls exchanged looks. Wanda made a face. Rose stifled her laughter. George turned right off the hallway and into their mother's bedroom. A few moments later he was off down the hallway, out the front door and into the clatter of the block of flats.

Rose leaned against the door jamb and gazed down the empty hall. It had never come to this. Not with Stan. Not even with Whoopsie. Oh, a weekend at the Katoomba motel, perhaps, or a few nights in a row there at the flat. But that's all it had been, a promise of impermanence collecting on their lives.

She wondered if her father would ever come home, wondered what he'd do, if he'd even care. He was off playing in a showband, touring Queensland in a Holden stationwagon. He'd been gone for months. He was probably eating papaya and drinking up lots of Four X. Bugger him, she thought. Why did he have to go off and leave us here?

She slid her hands into her jeans pockets. 'He said he comes from Tripoli.'

'Where's that?' said Wanda, who was standing at the cluttered vanity, pulling a brush through her hair.

'I don't know. Greece, I think. Maybe India.'

'No dummy. It's not India. He's not *Indian*. You mean Italian. It's probably Italy.'

'Nope,' said Rose, shaking her head.

'How would *you* know?' Wanda put down the brush and began to squeeze a pimple that hid in the crease of her chin.

'He hates spaghetti. He told me in the restaurant.'

'So?'

'So he's not Italian. Is he?'

'He might be. What'd he end up ordering?'

Rose glanced down the hall again. 'A hamburger with egg. Lots of chips. And a bottle of beer.'

'What kind?'

'Fosters.'

'Hmm,' said Wanda, squeezing harder. 'He never bought *me* a dress.'

'Well, you never wanted to come.' She turned to see him carrying in a beaten-up suitcase and an electric frying pan. A white towel hung around his neck and a roll of toilet paper was clamped in his armpit.

'He's got one of those pots you plug into the wall,' remarked Rose.

'Into the powerpoint?'

'Yeah. A big one.'

'Looks like he's gunna park his backside in here for a while, then.'

'I guess so.'

'I betcha.'

'I guess you're right.'

'Did you see what he cooked for breakfast this morning?' said Wanda. They were strolling down Darlinghurst Road, each sucking a Chup-a-chup. A skinny man eyed them from outside the Pink Pussycat, hands behind his back, feet apart, planted on the pavement like a soldier.

'No,' replied Rose. 'What was it?'

'It was —' Wanda turned and pulled a face at the man. He suddenly looked away. Rose giggled.

'I don't think it had a *name*,' continued Wanda. 'It was, like, *mush*. I told him, I told him, "We don't eat that. We eat Coco Pops for breakfast."'

'And what did he say?'

'He didn't say anything. He just sat down and ripped up all this flat bread stuff, and scooped up his *food* with it.' Wanda shook her head. 'Not a fork or a spoon. He just used the bread.'

They crossed Roslyn Street and both nodded to a woman in green satin hot pants who was leaning against a plate glass window. Rose often saw her there, often wondered why she hovered in the same spot every day, smiling at passers-by.

They walked by the Bourbon and Beefsteak — where all the American sailors got pissed after they docked in at Garden Island — and came to a doorway. They stepped down a flight of stairs, descending into a thick scent of incense and musk oil.

The Flea Market was always dimly lit. People were into candles down there, long fat candles, handmade and rainbow-coloured. One young bearded man had a booth and candles were all that he sold. He called his enterprise My Old Flame, and always had a candle in the shape of a woman's head burning on a wooden plant stand beside his stool.

Wanda was looking over the candles as though she might buy one. She'd already bought two in the last month, all in an effort to start a conversation with the man.

Rose wandered on, her eyes falling on silver puzzle rings mounted on deep purple velvet, tie-dyed T-shirts, a poster tacked to the wall that read, 'What If They Gave a War and Nobody Came?'

She dreamed herself into embroidered cheesecloth dresses and hand-made leather sandals, she fingered Indian love beads, she took a tiny crystal between her thumb and forefinger and held it up to a stained-glass lamp.

Carlos Santana's 'Evil Ways' began to a crackle over the PA system. A woman with dark, straight hair who had a tarot-card-reading booth began to dance alone behind her table.

The man at the leatherwork booth opposite stopped eating his Chinese takeaway and started tapping out a rhythm against the side of his workbench with a pair of wooden chopsticks.

Rose looked back to see Wanda hurrying up behind her. She placed the crystal back onto the display table. 'No more candles?'

'This woman came up to him,' hissed Wanda, 'and, and —'

'What?'

Wanda glanced back quickly. 'And kissed him. On the mouth. A *French* kiss.'

Rose stared back at her sister blankly. 'Are you gunna tell Mum?'

'Of course not, dummy. Why would I tell Mum?'

'I don't know. . .'

Wanda rested her hands on her hips and gazed down at Rose. 'You don't know what it is, do you?'

Rose bit her lip. 'I bet the French made it up.'

'Oh, *der* Rose,' replied Wanda. 'It's a sloppy kiss. Tongue 'n all. Like sucking an orange.'

They turned and continued strolling through the market.

'How would *you* know?' Rose was still considering whether to believe her sister.

'Because I've done it millions of times. With Lance. And Ricky. Ricky's the best.'

Rose thought of Ricky's pimpled face and grimaced. She stopped to touch a yellow silk scarf. She stroked a satin jacket, and maroon velvet shoulder bag. 'Want to go halves on a packet of incense?'

'What kind?'

'Strawberry?'

Wanda rolled her eyes.

'Um, what about sandalwood?'

'Nope,' said Wanda. 'Let's get patchouli. All the hip people get patchouli. We'll burn it in our room when I play my Deep Purple records.'

Wanda stood by the window in her blue and white Indian-print dress, counting up the coloured virgin bangles on her left wrist.

Rose stood on the other side of their bedroom and planted sticks of incense into a crack in the wall. She then struck a match and lit six of them, one by one, as if they were candles on a birthday cake.

'He put this painting up on the wall,' she remarked, 'of a rooster.'

'In the loungeroom,' said Wanda. 'I saw it. Anyway, it's not a painting. It's a, a *thing*.'

'You mean a print?'

'It's not a print. It's done on velvet. Imitation velvet. It's a velvet rooster.'

'It looks like him,' said Rose.

Wanda laughed and fell down on the bed. 'You're right. From now on, that's what we'll call him. The rooster.'

'The *velvet* rooster.' Rose fell down next to her sister.

When they had stopped laughing, she lay on her back across the bed and let her head hang over the side. Wanda sat on a pillow at the head of the bed and clipped her toenails. Deep Purple's 'Smoke on the Water' droned in the background like a recurring daydream.

'Ricky's got a car now,' announced Wanda. 'He just got his licence. His dad gave him his old beetle.'

'Does it work?'

'Of course it works. And one day we're gunna drive all over Australia.'

'Bull.'

'We are! Me and him and Shelley and Spud.'

'All in a beetle?'

'Spud's saving up to buy a Falcon.'

'What'll you do? Live with the Aborigines?'

'Maybe. We could live off wild pineapple. We could go apple picking. We could swim in the nude and drink beer 'til dawn everyday if we wanted.'

'Mum wouldn't let you.'

'Mum?' Wanda snorted. 'Who cares about Mum? Mum's doing what she wants to, isn't she? So's Dad! Ned's pissed off and is living in a, an attic, and playing in a rock band. And, and the *rooster*,' she stammered, pointing to the door, 'the velvet rooster is sitting back in Dad's chair and drinking up the last of Dad's Bundaberg rum! So don't tell me what Mum won't let me do. I can do anything I want.'

'If I had my choice,' said Rose, 'I'd live in Greenwich Village and play the piano all day. And I'd paint pictures. Paintings. And I'd sell them on the street for money.'

'Where's Greenwich Village?'

'Somewhere in America. Dad told me about it. He said the

cafés stay open all night long. And the black people play the best music in the world in the clubs 'til five o'clock in the morning, and they serve you cup after cup of coffee and you only pay for one.'

'I heard they kill people over there.'

Rose rolled over and looked up at her sister. 'No they don't. They don't. You're thinking of Africa. In America they sell paintings on the street and the black people play the best music all night long. It'd be better than picking apples. It'd be better than staying *here*.'

Rose sat up and stretched. The record player clicked and the arm lifted and returned. The corners of Wanda's mouth drooped and they both turned towards the window and peered out, out into the laneway that was always dotted with metal garbage cans and stray, hungry cats.

They had wandered up to Macleay Street, to the Fitzroy Gardens, and would have sat by the El Alamein Fountain, but it was not running. It looked as if someone had poured in bottles of red dye the night before. Dark, scarlet water stagnated at the bottom of the fountain like a big sore at the edge of the park.

Instead, they pursued a path, slinking past a woman asleep on a bench, who was blanketed up to her neck with pages from the *Sydney Morning Herald*. Green fronds fanned up over beds of snapdragons and buttercups. On the expanse of green grass in the park's center sat a circle of Aborigines and a white man and woman. An older, bearded Aboriginal man reclined on one elbow; a woman was rocking back, laughing. A skinny youth, not as dark as the others, but with a shock of thick, black hair, passed a flagon of wine along to the white woman.

The two sisters sat on a wooden bench facing the grass. Wanda crossed her legs. Rose tied a loose shoelace. The old Aboriginal man slid his elbow forward and stretched out flat on his back.

Both sat without saying a word and watched the flagon change hands. A tiny, frail man, whose loose trousers slid down over his bare, white buttocks, tottered by pushing a wheelbarrow with Department of Main Roads sprayed on the side in red. In it were a few bits of clothing, a green plastic lampshade, a straw broom, and a black army boot. Lumps of dry cement still clung to the rim. A dirty white bow tie hung from one wooden handle. The man steered the wheelbarrow right and trundled off over the grass to join the circle.

Rose looked across her shoulder and eyed a woman leaning up against the brick wall of the library. A pair of fat legs extended out from under a pink lamé minidress. Her shoes were a pair of scuffed, patent leather pumps. Her makeup was thick and gaudy.

'*She's* ugly, isn't she?' whispered Rose.

Wanda turned and looked. The woman was searching through a beaded shoulder bag. She finally produced a cigarette and lit it up.

'That's a *man*, you drongo,' hissed Wanda. 'Can't you tell?'

Rose's eyebrows arched. She glanced at her sister and then back at the pink dress, the high heels, the cigarette, watched the way full, red lips blew out a puff of smoke.

'But she's got big bosoms,' insisted Rose. 'Bigger than your two fried eggs.'

'That's what I mean,' Wanda whispered. '*Real* women don't have boobs that big.'

'They're falsettos?'

'Falsies, Rose,' replied Wanda. 'They're called falsies.'

Rose glanced back at the pink lamé. 'Why would any man want to be a woman?'

Wanda shrugged.

'If I were a man,' announced Rose, 'I wouldn't want to be a woman. I'd rather be a man any day. They get to do anything they like.'

The two sisters gazed across as a man in a faded pair of jeans and a black tailcoat approached the pink lamé. They began to exchange words, were smiling at each other. The pink lamé took the black tailcoat's hand and they drifted off together, through the humid green of January, like a tainted Fred and Ginger.

'I don't mind being a girl,' said Wanda, combing her hair back with her fingers. 'I like wearing dresses. And nailpolish. The trouble with you, Rose —' she tilted her face up to meet the sun, '— is that you're not old enough. Wait 'til you lose some of that baby fat, you'll see.'

Rose straightened and crossed her arms. 'Well, you're not exactly, um, Miss Australia, you know.'

'No,' agreed Wanda, still holding her face up to the sun. 'I'm more like Miss Universe. And you,' she added, 'you're more like Miss —' she looked across at Rose '— Miss Toongabbie.'

Rose blushed. '*You're* more like Miss —' she tried to think of somewhere really awful '— Miss Woy Woy.'

'You're more like Miss Yakandandah.'

'Miss Back-of-Bourke.'

Wanda pursed her lips. 'Miss The-Rotten-Side-of-Redfern.'

'Miss Elephant's Bum.'

'Miss, Miss Kangaroo, Miss Kangaroo Shit!'

The two caught each other in a moment of hesitation. They heard the wheelbarrow man cry out, 'Gis another swig, you bludgers!' A plump, middle-aged woman was on her feet, in the centre of the circle, shaking her upper body and singing 'Lucy in the Sky With Diamonds'. A breeze swept up from Rushcutters Bay. The two girls began to laugh. They stood up and wandered down the path, arm-in-arm.

'You're not really gunna go, are you?' said Rose, as she slid open her box of Derwents.

'Why?'

Rose's fingers rummaged through the box. 'I'd be all by myself. Just me and Mum and, you know, the rooster.'

'He likes you better than me. He hates me.' Wanda was sitting in a lotus position on the floor of their bedroom with eyes closed and hands upturned, resting on her knees.

'No he doesn't, Wan.' Rose picked up a red pencil and drew a half circle in her scrapbook. 'He said, he said, just the other day that you had nice teeth. He said um —' her face tightened into an imitation of George's serious frown and she announced in a stilted monotone '— that Wanda, she got real good teeth!'

Wanda opened her eyes. 'All the better to eat him with.'

'Shh! He might hear you.'

'I don't care.' Wanda closed her eyes again. 'I'm meditating. *Nothing* disturbs me when I'm meditating. I don't care what he thinks. He carries on like Adolph-bloody-Hitler. He never lets me play my records when he's home. The other day he told me to shut up. He even reads my mail!'

'What mail?' said Rose, putting down the red and picking up the yellow. 'You never get any mail.'

Wanda drew in a long breath. 'Ricky left me a note on the door the other day.'

'*That's* not mail.'

'It is. It sort of is,' retorted Wanda. 'It's a —' she pressed her palms together in a prayer position '— an invasion of privacy.'

Rose put down the green and picked up the grey. She scribbled a sky across the top of the page. 'I wish Dad'd come home.'

'Dad's not coming home. He's never coming home. Don't you understand that? You heard the blue they had before he left.'

'But —'

'He's not coming back, Rose. You'll just have to cop it.'

Rose sighed. She put down the grey and picked up the yellow. She pressed down hard, drawing a long, thick line until the lead broke. She flung it back into the box and looked across at her sister. 'Won't you miss me?'

Without opening her eyes, Wanda nodded to the door. 'I won't miss *him*.'

'But *me*?'

'I suppose I will.'

Rose smiled to herself and picked up the red again.

'But I won't miss your farts,' added Wanda, looking up.

Rose paused and met her gaze. Wanda looked ridiculous sitting there with her legs all tied up in a knot. Rose bit on the end of the pencil. She tried to suppress the grin that was slipping across her face.

They knew they shouldn't have. They knew it was wrong. It was Wanda's idea. It was over-the-line. It would cause a stink. They would regret it.

It seemed pretty harmless at first. Wanda kept saying that it would be just for an hour, that their mother and the rooster would never know. She kept saying that they'd be gone for ages, out at their party in Little Lebanon, and Rose went along with it for the sake of Wanda.

Wanda tied her purple halter top around Rose's neck and back and handed her a pair of long, silver, heart-shaped earrings. She then insisted that Rose put on her Levis and handed her a belt with a brass buckle.

They scuffled through their mother's makeup. They coloured their lips Misty Pink and Flaming Red. Wanda showed her how to pluck her eyebrows and it hurt. They splashed on the rooster's Brut and suddenly cried out 'Cock-a-doodle-doo!' and strutted around in a circle. Wanda pulled on their mother's black satin dress. It was too big, so she snatched up a red sash that went with the rooster's dressing gown and tied it around her waist. Rose burrowed through the jewellery box and handed her a string of pearls and kept a long gold chain for herself. Wanda then grabbed her mother's only two hats: the 1940s black one with the feather and veil went on her own head, while the white cowgirl Stetson was propped upon Rose's.

They looked like a stunted Annie Oakley and Tallulah Bankhead as they paraded up Springfield Avenue. It was around eight-thirty when they got to Darlinghurst Road. They stopped and considered which way to go: right was all the strip clubs and pinball parlours; left was the souvenir shops, tatoo joints, Kentucky Fried Chicken, the fountain. Across the street was Les Girls, the bright red neon light pulsing on and off like a stop sign after midnight.

They ended up sipping cappucinos in the window seat of Sweethearts, pretending they were in Paris. Wanda leaned across her cup and said, 'Bon *jaw*.' Rose didn't know any French so she told Wanda to get fucked in Italian. The coffee was milky and sweet and had three teaspoons of sugar and lots of chocolate on top. The sound system piped out 'Lady Be Good' and Rose bobbed up and down in her seat to it while Wanda spouted out all the French words she knew, including numbers up to ten. As Rose swayed and tapped her foot, as she looked at Wanda pronouncing 'Polly voo, polly voo,' over and over again, she wondered how long it would be, how much time they had left, and suddenly stopped jigging up and down.

Outside, two sailors in white suits sauntered by. They glanced in through the plate-glass window. Rose poked her tongue out and

Wanda blew them a kiss. The sailors laughed. One pulled his cap off and held it to his chest. He stood in front of Wanda and mouthed, *I love you.*

Wanda bit her lip and shook her head. The sailor squeezed his cap; *I love you*, he mouthed again. His friend was still laughing. Wanda frowned and made a shooing motion with her hand. *Really*, he mouthed, knees bent, hands clenched, *I love you!* He pointed to his chest and then at Wanda. His friend was doubling over. Wanda leaned closer to the glass and slowly lifted her veil. Rose tilted across also. The sailor lowered his head to meet Wanda at eye level. *Piss off*, mouthed Wanda. The sailor straightened up. Wanda raised two fingers at him.

The sailor's face tightened. 'What the hell!' he shouted through the glass. 'You're ugly anyway!' Before he walked away he turned and poked out his tongue at Rose.

Rose straightened her hat. 'Whad you do that for?'

'What?'

'Give 'em the finger 'n all.'

'All sailors,' remarked Wanda, 'have got diseases. Didn't you know?'

'No,' mumbled Rose. 'I didn't.'

'Well they do. Ones you can't cure. I thought everyone knew that.'

Rose shrugged. 'I thought they looked nice. White suits and everything.'

Wanda put down her coffee cup. 'When,' she said, lowering her veil, 'are you going to grow up?'

Darlinghurst Road swelled with people. Crowds combed the footpath. The evening was suspended in neon light and snatches of jazz from basement bars.

They stood outside a fish and chip shop and looked across the street at the Pink Pussycat. It looked more exciting in the evening. The front was painted bright pink and had a line of flashing lightbulbs around the entrance. On either side of the doorway was a mural of two naked women with cat's ears and a tail that curled around ankles. A chubby man in a black suit and bow tie stood on a wooden box out the front. The right side of his face was completely clean-shaven while the left sported exactly one half of a sandy-coloured beard and moustache.

'Live striptease!' he cried. 'Women *and* men. Get it while it's hot!' He slapped the side of the box with a black cane for emphasis. 'We got gorgeous sheilas and randy blokes. We got turn-ons for all you folks.'

Rose took a step closer to Wanda. Wanda crossed her arms and continued to gaze across the street. He was attracting a small group of onlookers and gestured to the flashing entranceway and the first few steps of a flight of stairs.

'Let's get some chips,' said Rose.

'How much money you got?'

'Eighty-one cents.'

Wanda lifted her veil. 'Let's get a battered sav.'

'A chiko roll.'

Wanda glanced into the store. 'What about a pie?'

'Eighty-one cents . . .' murmured Rose. 'Scallops. Let's get scallops. Twelve cents each. Two of us. That's um —' She slid her hands into her pockets.

'Six twelves are seventy two,' announced Wanda, already sweeping into the shop, 'and two threes are six. Let's get scallops.'

They followed their usual route along Macleay Street, came to 31 Flavours, crossed the road and wandered back down the other side. Rose loved to slide her hands inside the warm bag of scallops encased in layers of butcher paper and racing pages from the *Daily Telegraph*. It felt like a steaming, oversized mitten around her hand. The scallops were too hot to eat but she bit into them anyway. Salty, battered potato against her tongue, the illuminated fountain, the high-heeled crowd, the lights, the rush of Saturday night: it was enough; it was plenty. It didn't hurt when a tissue of skin fell away from the roof of her mouth.

But Wanda suddenly stopped and said she had to call Ricky. She insisted that Rose stand out in front of Kentucky Fried Chicken and wait for her.

'But there's no more money,' said Rose. 'Eighty-one cents. That was it.'

Wanda hitched up the black satin dress. 'I've got a five-cent piece.'

Rose crossed her arms. 'We coulda got another scallop!'

'Rose, shut up.' Wanda turned. 'I got to call Ricky.' She disappeared into the chicken store and left Rose out the front. Rose was disappointed; she wanted to listen in. She leaned against the wall and surveyed the street. She felt good standing out there with the big hat on her head. Crowds swarmed by and stared at her. A sailor whistled. A man entering the store bent down and said she looked adorable. Rose liked being adorable. She liked being stared at. Perhaps that's why the woman in the green hotpants always hung about on the corner.

Wanda emerged a few minutes later, smiling. 'Come on, cowboy,' she said, pulling the hat down over Rose's face, 'let's go this way.'

They wandered back down the street, away from the fountain. Rose wanted to ask questions, to say something, but she couldn't force out a word. Wanda stepped a little ahead, the feather in her hat bouncing up and down, and Rose noticed a wiggle, a kind of sashay settling into her sister's walk.

They saw a crowd gathered on the next corner, outside the ANZ bank, and dashed across the street to find an old man playing a cello. He was seated on a wooden stool, dressed in a well-worn grey three-piece suit and burgundy tie. Round wire-rimmed glasses were perched at the tip of his nose while tiny budgerigars wandered in circles at his feet, pecking at the ground.

Suddenly, he stopped playing and lowered his bow to the ground and a budgie hopped on. He continued with his sonata, the budgie still clinging to the bow like a nervous child on a rollercoaster. The crowd clapped; the cello sighed and groaned. The smell of approaching rain swept across the corner.

The two girls watched the crowd rise and fall. They tossed tiny pieces of potato to the birds and went across the street to buy a cup of tea for the man when he asked them to. Soon they had learnt the name of each budgie: Charlie, Elizabeth, Anne, Edward, and Andrew. The man's name was Rupert. Rose wondered how he could tell the birds apart. They were all yellow and green, all had the same little squeaky chirp.

He let Rose hold them in her hands while he played. The crowd grew; people craned their necks and pushed in front of each other. Wanda stood out the front with her mother's black hat upturned and began to slip from person to person, muttering something about her grandfather needing an operation.

Rupert continued to play with one budgie on his bow, while Rose swayed from side to side, suspended in the cello's deep vowel sounds. The tickle of tiny bird feet crossed her palms and she felt the warmth of scores of people who stood around watching.

He stopped playing again and, instead of extending the bow to her outstretched hand, raised it and pointed it upwards. The budgie slipped off the bow and onto the white cowgirl hat and everyone laughed. They congregated around Wanda and dropped in money, and one man stepped up to Rose and tucked a two dollar bill into her front jeans pocket.

Rupert started in on a faster melody and Rose began to dance from one foot to the other while balancing the birds and smiling at the audience. For a moment, all she was conscious of was the mixed sensation of music and flashing lights, the budgies' staccato chirps blending with car horns and the sound of change dropping into the hat.

She was doing little side-steps in a half-circle when she saw Wanda abruptly swing around. Her sister's eyes widened and she looked as if she might scream. Wanda ran across to Rupert's cello case and dropped in all the money.

'Come *on*!' she cried. 'Now!'

Rose was frozen. She had three birds in her hands and one on her hat.

'Rose, come *on*!' yelled Wanda.

Rupert stopped playing. The crowd began to murmur.

'Put down the birds, idiot! Hurry!'

Wanda snatched up the one on Rose's hat and put it on the ground. Rose bent down and let the others go.

Wanda grabbed her by the hand and began pulling her through the crowd.

'Bye Mister —' cried Rose, struggling to look back '— Rupert. Thank you for —'

Wanda wrenched her off the curb and pulled her across the road before oncoming traffic. A car tooted; somebody shouted. The cello's low moan started up again.

She could see the outline of Wanda's body through the darkness, her chest rising and falling with each breath, feet sticking out from beneath a white sheet. All that filled the emptiness between them was the sniffle of Rose's short gasps for air. She rolled onto her side to face her sister's bed and curled up into a ball.

'I'm sorry, Wan.' Rose waited for the edge of a voice to cut through the darkness, but nothing surfaced, not even a movement.

'I said I was sorry.' All she heard was the distant wail of a siren. 'I am, Wan. Really.'

'Shut up.'

Rose sniffed and felt blood rise to her face. The bite of the belt still burned her legs.

'You,' continued Wanda, 'are the biggest idiot *dag* I've ever met.'

'But they knew anyway. They —'

'They didn't know. You only *thought* they knew.'

'Well they woulda found out.'

'Yeah, because of your big fat mouth.'

Rose drew the bedspread up over her shoulder. She saw Wanda turn over.

'But they *saw* us.'

Wanda sighed. 'I saw *them*. They were coming out of Les Girls. Who said anything about them seeing us? You know what?' Wanda's voice rose a fraction. 'You'd have to be the dumbest thing walking around on two legs. A cockroach'd have to be smarter than you.'

'I was scared,' gushed Rose, 'of the rooster. He yelled at me and —'

'I was there, you dummy! I saw the way you started bawling your brains out like a baby. He hit me — you know — he hit me harder than you. And I didn't start bawling. I didn't carry on like a bloody *baby*.'

Rose said nothing. There was never anything to say after Wanda had made a remark like that. It would be better tomorrow. She would do something for Wanda: brush her hair, make her some tea, paint her nails, imitate the rooster, pay her penance.

Sleep was coming quickly. Her eyelids grew as heavy as her

desire for morning. Neon lights flashed across a white coffee cup. Day-glo musical notes danced through a black doorway. A man wrapped his arms around a telegraph pole and kissed it. Green turned to yellow and yellow to orange and orange changed to red. A waterfall poured out of the Crest Hotel, spilling out of high windows and flooding the street with blue waves that lapped up onto shopfronts and double-decker buses.

What was it that moved? Something dragged. Something click-ed. Was it the man? Was it still night? Did something move? Was it her?

Rose looked up: it was a figure. A figure was by the window. The window was sliding up. She blinked. It was Wanda. Wanda was slipping out. It was Wanda slipping out of the window. Rose opened her mouth. She could cry out. She could have her mother in here in a second. Wanda was disappearing. What had gone wrong? She could scream. She could stop it. Nothing came out. She was frozen. Wanda was gone and Rose still couldn't move and still didn't speak and all she saw was the darkness of the room.

7

A RED TRAIN TO THE PEOPLE'S PALACE

Rose didn't know what to expect as she stood outside the lime-green weatherboard house. Would he be home from work already? Would she be there? Would she be awake? Sober? Would she notice Rose had lost her navy-blue felt school hat?

Yes, she would notice. Her mother always noticed what was not there: a hat, a belt, money, a husband. Rose knew her mother hid a list of losses somewhere in between the memory of the separation and the day she met him.

Tiptoeing down the hallway, she saw that her mother's bedroom door was closed. Rose put down her school case and headed for the kitchen. George's car wasn't in the driveway. Good, she thought. Very good. Rose thought of what had happened the night before and hoped he would never come home.

Her mother was probably taking a nap. Rose turned, stiffened momentarily, and hurried over to the medicine cabinet above the sink. She pushed aside the cough medicine, the bottle of mylanta, and snatched up the serepax and valium. She peered into the pale orange plastic containers. The pills were all still there.

'Rosie?!'

She put them back on the shelf and shut the cupboard door. Rose hurried through the livingroom, back into the hallway, and opened the bedroom door.

She found her mother slouched on the bed, frowning, a cigarette between her fingers. The deep purple bruises were still there, looking like a teaspoon of Indian ink dropped onto blotting paper. Rose noticed her mother's feeble attempt at masking the diagonal cut across her forehead and the bluish swelling that bloomed across her right eye: a thick layer of makeup, and her fair hair brushed down into a fringe.

The long cigarette ash suddenly dropped onto her mother's polyester slacks.

'OK, Rose,' she said, standing up and straightening her crumpled cotton blouse. There was a slight shake in her voice. 'We're getting out of here.'

Rose gazed at her blankly. She could smell the brandy on her mother's breath.

'We're getting out,' her mother repeated. 'Now come on, quick! Get out of your uniform and put a change of clothes in your school case.'

'But where —'

'Just do it. I got my cheque today. Hurry up before he gets home.'

Her mother swung her around and guided her into the hallway.

Standing in front of her wardrobe, Rose flung off her uniform and stood in her underpants, unable to decide what to put on or what to take.

'Come *on*,' her mother cried from the hallway.

At once Rose pulled out a pink velvet party dress, gathered at the neck with white frills, and put it on. Black leather patent shoes. She left her white school socks on. What else? She heard her mother cough outside. Rose grabbed a book, *Island of the Blue Dolphin*, from her table and rushed back into the hallway.

She found her mother wearing a large pair of dark sunglasses and clinging to a vinyl overnight bag. The front door was slammed shut and they half-ran down Berith Street, still holding onto each other, Rose struggling to keep up with her mother's urgent stride. With every moment they were met with another suburban home to hurry by: garden gnomes and deck chairs, hedges trimmed into cat shapes. He'd be home soon. He'd look for them.

'We getting the train, Mum?'

Her mother nodded.

Rose clutched her book with her free hand. 'You know where we're going?'

'Yes.'

They turned left and headed down Shaw Street. The station was ahead of them. About five minutes away. Soon, Rose thought.

When they stepped down to cross Caroline Street they saw him, in his white 1968 Holden. Driving past them. On his way home. She felt her mother's grip tighten around her hand. Felt her stop breathing. Stiffen.

Her mother looked about wildly, like an animal seeking camouflage. The car tried to turn against oncoming traffic.

Telegraph poles and fences shot by as they ran into the wind, towards the Catholic church further up the block.

They flung themselves into the monastic silence between two pews of the third and fourth row, near the altar. Her mother pressed a finger to her lips and her eyebrows narrowed. Rose lay down on her stomach and stared across the floor of the church, anticipating the appearance of his heavy work boots.

They waited for several minutes. Her mother was on her knees, crouched over, not daring to look up. Rose gazed at the coloured light filtering through a stained-glass window, the deep reds and blues reaching down towards them. God through glass, she thought.

Her mother had insisted on sending her to religious instruction since kindergarten, and Rose had made her first Holy Communion in a white lace dress. She was the top student of her religious class. But lying there on the wooden floor, with a gripping coldness penetrating her, Rose thought God was about as real as the coloured light, only existing on the inside of the church. Outside, it was always the same.

She heard her mother fishing through the overnight bag and turned to see her unscrewing the top of a flask of McWilliam's brandy. She took a quick sip and a deep breath, and then whispered, 'OK, Rose, let's sneak out the side way.'

They both crawled to the end of the pew and dashed out the door closest to the altar. The street's inevitable hum — of cars and voices — enveloped them as they raced to catch the four-fifteen train into town.

Rose wished they could have caught a fast, modern, silver train, a double-decker one that could speed them away from Kingsgrove as fast as a granted wish. Instead they found themselves on green leather seats in an ancient red train, one that would stop at every western suburb, and slowly rattle past the milk bars, pubs and football ovals that flanked the railway line into town.

'You OK, Luv?' Her mother lit up a Viscount as the train jerked forward and pulled out of the station.

'We got away all right, didn't we?'

'Yep. Like to see him catch up with us now.'

They both smiled.

'Mum?'

'Mmm?'

'You got your cheque today?'

'Yes.'

'Where are we going to go?'

'Into town.'

'I know. But *where* into town?'

'How would you like to go and stay in a nice hotel?'

Rose began pinching the velvet hem of her dress.

'Wouldn't you like that, Rose?'

'Where is it?'

'In town. Oh, it's a nice place. You'll like it. It's called The People's Palace.'

Rose thought of Buckingham Palace, Windsor Palace, the palace in *Cinderella*. Marble staircases. Chandeliers. Crystal champagne glasses.

As they pulled into Bexley North station, she glanced up at the advertisements above the windows of the carriage: the paddle-pop lion with a new banana flavour, and a woman with dark long hair holding a bottle of Revlon liquid makeup. A man's hand lay on her shoulder and she was smiling.

She looked across at her mother, at her mother's makeup. Rose could see, around the corners of her mouth, an accumulation of years, a cluster of tiny miseries nothing could erase.

Rose had worn makeup twice. Wanda had painted it on both times. That was before she ran away. Like their mother, Wanda was beautiful. Her hair wasn't thin and unruly, like Rose's. It was thick and fair, almost white, catching light as it framed her face.

Rose missed Wanda, the things Wanda would do for her, like the day with the makeup. She remembered how Wanda had unbraided her long plaits, the brush easing through her hair, anticipating every touch, every stroke, the feather-weight of her hands. She remembered how the powder smelt like African violets, the moistness of the burgundy lipstick, how she had to be still for the mascara, had to stare at a spot on the wall.

Later, Wanda took Rose to Luna Park and paid fifty cents to have photos taken in an automatic booth.

'See?' Wanda had said, after the photos had dropped down the chute. 'See how beautiful you are?'

And Rose had seen herself looking years older, defined features, no freckles, lips slightly pouted like Wanda had shown her. Yes she did, she did look beautiful. She looked different and beautiful. But Rose realised, as she sat on the train, gazing out over the factories of Camperdown, with every detail blurred by an infinite greyness, that she didn't crave to be beautiful any more.

As the train rumbled close to the heart of the city, Rose caught a glimpse of Australia Square, high and round, towering above Sydney's skyline. She saw the Central Station clock looming over the city. Five-past-five.

'People's Palace,' she whispered under her breath.

They got off at Central Station with a swarm of other people and headed down a flight of stairs. Each step Rose took under the city's glare seemed to her a game of blind man's bluff: unsure, new territory, not trusting the eyes and hands that guided her.

They headed east through Belmore Park as the sun set behind them. The half-light of dusk hung above the evergreens. Rose tried not to stare at the bodies wrapped in rags, the empty metho bottles. She tried not to see the bird droppings on the sleeve of an old woman's cardigan, tried not to hear a bearded man talking to his flagon of port. She felt her mother's grip tighten again as they hurried to the edge of Chinatown.

The roads were cluttered with cars, people elbowing their way out of the city. Rose and her mother darted around roadworks and headed up Pitt Street, leaving behind red lanterns, fluorescent flags and the deafening stutter of a jackhammer.

'How far, Mum?' Rose didn't like this part of town. She liked the harbour side better, the ferries, the Opera House, the sandstone buildings, the smell of salt water and toffee apples at Circular Quay.

'Just a couple of blocks,' her mother assured her. 'Nearly there. Goodness!' she continued. 'You must be getting hungry. Haven't had your tea or anything.'

'Mmm...a bit,' said Rose, who was more eager to get to the People's Palace.

On the next corner, however, Rose's mother stopped at a pub and bought a fifth of McWilliam's brandy and a meat pie with tomato sauce from the snack bar.

Rose said nothing the moment she saw marble turn into stained linoleum, crystal into plastic, chandeliers shrink to dusty yellow light globes. Inside the foyer of the People's Palace it was dim and damp, a layer of dark green paint flaked off the wall; the wooden clock above the desk had stopped at 3:12. Rose found herself looking up at a balding, scowling man who slouched against a coke machine, while her mother arranged for a room.

The old, creaking lift stopped at the fifth floor. Rose's mother pulled back the iron gate and they stepped out onto brown, threadbare carpet that seemed to go on forever down a long, narrow hallway.

Every door they passed was identical, placed evenly apart, and there seemed to be no end to them.

They stopped in front of room 533. Her mother pushed the key in the lock, turned, and flung open the door. She turned on the light by pulling a string.

At once Rose noticed another dusty yellow light globe that hung from the centre of the ceiling. Then she noticed the two narrow iron beds, like old-fashioned hospital beds. The walls were off-white, stained from years of cigarette smoke.

'Come on, Rosie.' Her mother guided Rose to a metal chair behind the door. 'Sit down and eat your pie before it gets cold.'

'Mum, what are we going to do now?'

'Eat your pie.'

'But where do we go?'

'Tomorrow. I'll tell you tomorrow.'

'Are we ever going back?'

'No...maybe.' Her mother removed the sunglasses and folded them, shaking her head. 'Maybe to get our things.'

Rose wondered what her mother was thinking as they lay on their beds in the darkness. She could see her silhouette, her profile against the frame of the open window, the hand occasionally reaching out to the bedside table and the head tilting to take a sip.

She heard her cough; heard the flush of the toilet from the bathroom down the hall; but mostly she heard the monotone of silence.

'Rose?' Her mother was still lying on her back, staring out the window.

'Yes?'

'Rose. I'm going to die. Tonight. I'm going to die tonight.'

Rose sat up. 'No! You're not! What —'

'I am.' Her mother's voice was low and serious, like an television newsreader reporting an earthquake. 'I know I am. Rose, I'm dying.'

Rose jumped out of her own bed and sat down beside her, rocking, rocking her back and forth. She felt her mother's body tremble within the circle of her arms, warm tears against her neck.

'No, Mum,' she whispered, now trying to convince them both. 'You're not dying. You're not gunna die.'

'Yes I —'

Rose continued rocking, kissing her forehead. 'You're not gunna die.'

'Yes I *am*! I *am*.' Her mother rolled over sideways and drew her knees up to hug them.

'Do you have a pain, Mum?' Rose reached closer. '*Mum*?'

'My whole damn life!'

She's not going to die, Rose told herself. She's not. She can't. She can't die now. Rose suddenly saw herself alone and lost in the middle of the city with nothing but her pink velvet party dress.

She sat on the edge of her mother's bed, holding her hand and stroking her forehead until her mother finally fell asleep. She then tiptoed back to her own bed and lay, listening to her mother's drunken breathing, making sure it continued, continued with its slow, heavy rhythm until light edged a path across the brick wall and fell into the room.

They ate their breakfast in silence at the milk bar across the street. Tea and toast. Her mother had only the tea. Rose had decided not to ask any more questions.

'How would you like to go and see a movie this morning?' her mother said.

Rose looked up. The sunglasses and makeup were on again. 'Which one?'

Her mother got up and bought a copy of the *Sydney Morning Herald*. She thumbed through it and found the entertainment section.

'Pick any one you like!' she said, handing Rose the paper.

Putting down her teacup, Rose roved the movie page uneasily, wondering why her mother had chosen to see a film.

'*Storm Boy*,' she declared.

'All right,' replied her mother, '*Storm Boy*.'

'No hang on. No, *Picnic at Hanging Rock*.'

'*Picnic at Hanging Rock*?'

'Yes.'

'What time is the first session? Eleven?'

'Umm...Yes. Eleven. Eleven o'clock at the Hoyts.'

Rose's eyes swung from the popcorn machine and glared down at the bright purple carpet as they stood beside the ticket box.

'But I thought you were coming too!' she wailed.

'Rose, I'm going for a walk. *I* don't want to see a movie.' Her mother took out a handkerchief from the vinyl bag and blew her nose.

'But you were the one who thought of it!'

'I thought of it because I thought *you* would like to see a movie.'

Rose fidgeted with her right braid. 'Where are you going?'

'I told you. I'm going for a walk. Now look, it finishes at one o'clock. After it's over I'll meet you right here.'

'You'll be here when I come out?'

'At one o'clock. I promise.'

Rose's mother leant down and pecked her on the cheek. 'So run along now.' She motioned Rose to the usherette. 'Get yourself a good seat.'

In the anonymous darkness of the cinema, Rose gripped the arms of her seat and fixed her eyes upon the advertisements flashing across the screen. She wondered if they'd have to go back to the Palace, or if they'd end up going back on the red train to Kingsgrove, back to him, as they had so many times before.

Rose was distracted from everything when the music began. It was a flute, a melodic spell drawing her into the countryside upon the screen. She forgot where she was and became one of the beautiful schoolgirls at Appleyard College, dressed in a white cotton chemise, brushing her long hair as she gazed through white lace curtains. She was seduced by the high ceilings, the arched columns of the school, the way the girls stood in a row, lacing up each other's corsets, how Sarah pressed flowers into her notebook, the heavy, mahogany furniture, the blue and gold wallpaper. She could smell the bouquets of roses, feel the smooth railing of the grand staircase, and she listened intently when Miranda, the blonde girl, said 'What we see

and what we've seen

is but a dream

is but a dream.'

And when the girls made their way to Hanging Rock in a horsedrawn carriage, when they spread out their blanket and cut their heart-shaped, pink and white cake, when the clocks stopped and the cicadas' persistent drone took over, Rose was there. She was there, walking with them, leaping over streams, winding through gum trees, dodging goannas. She was sweating with them, exploring with them, with them as they fell under the land's hypnotic grip. She was there when Miranda said, 'Everything begins and ends at exactly the right time and place.' And when they disappeared, seemingly into the rock, consumed by the rock, consumed by the rock that would never return them, Rose went with them, happily.

She stood outside the theatre, clutching the hem of her dress and alternately looking up and down George Street as though she was watching a tennis match.

It was twenty minutes past one. She felt a dull ache inside, the pressure between her hips. She needed desperately to go to the toilet but didn't dare move. She pressed the inside of her legs together and bobbed up and down, crying, not caring. It was now one-thirty. The morning of lace and flutes and wildflowers had been broken. Her mother would never come back to pick her up. Her mother didn't want her, had abandoned her. Rose raised her hands to her face, her crying muted by the tenacious mumble of the city.

'Rosie! What's the matter?'

She grabbed her mother's hand. 'Where have you *been*?'

'Oh, I know I'm a little late, Rose.' Rose could smell beer. 'I'm sorry.' They began walking down George Street. 'I just got talking, you know.'

'Mum?'

'And I've got a surprise for you.'

'But —'

'Now, don't worry. We don't have to go back to the People's Palace.'

'It's just that I have to go —'

'Now let's cross the street while we've got the lights.'

Rose followed her mother across the road and into the corner pub on the other side.

The loud garble of the bar greeted them. Rose heard a radio spitting out the voice of an excited man calling a horse race over Perry Como crooning from the jukebox.

Her mother led her to a corner table.

'Rose,' she declared, 'this is Clarence.'

Rose blinked and waited for her eyes to adjust from the glare of the street. The race finished and the men at the bar were cheering. She looked up to see a man grinning down at her. His two bottom teeth were missing.

'Clarence,' she heard her mother say, 'is going to take us home. We're going to go and live with Clarence now.'

Rose saw the brown strands of hair growing out of his nose, the tattooed wreath on his right arm, the folds of fat gathered beneath his chin, and suddenly felt the sensation of warm liquid running down her legs.

8

FESTIVAL

Didi was driving and Fiona sat beside her eating a peach. Rose sat in the back seat, fiddling with the charm bracelet her mother had given her. She fingered the tiny, golden wishing well, felt the miniature cottage between her thumb and index finger. Next the tennis racket, the teacup, and then the old-fashioned bicycle with the bigger front wheel. Rose knew their order without looking, what came next and how far along the chain it was. And, as she gazed at Didi's hair — dyed blonde and styled into a crewcut — and Fiona's — dark, straight, and pulled back into a pony tail — and as she saw Fiona throw the peach stone out the window, felt the car stop at an intersection, as she saw the two women look at each other, turn, and kiss, kiss slowly, a hand on a knee, fingers to a cheek, as she heard a car horn blow behind them, saw them both pull away, laughing, Rose pressed each lucky charm between her fingers like a rosary.

All she knew was that they were taking her away for the Australia Day weekend. They said it was a festival in the country. Rose's mother thought it would be good for her to get away for a couple of days, for they had both been staying at the Women's Shelter for a week, unable to set a foot outside for fear that he'd be there waiting for them, waiting to take them back home.

She'd never seen them kiss before, she thought, as the car turned right into Parramatta Road and headed west. Other times at the shelter, times before this one, she'd noticed an arm on a shoulder or around a waist, a hug, a brief embrace. She'd noticed the overalls, the cropped hair, the way they rolled their own cigarettes from Drum tobacco. But Rose and her mother had never discussed the differences. They were good women, had always taken them in after he had beaten them up. They never accepted money. They were always there.

Past the factories of Camperdown, they hummed by Stanmore's Greek delicatessens, Italian milk bars, cheap Chinese restaurants, and old, tiled pubs already brimming with people eager to celebrate the long weekend; Rose noticed some even spilled out onto the footpath or sat on steps outside and drank schooners.

'Bloody hell.' Didi slapped the dashboard as the car crawled along the outside lane. 'I knew we should've left earlier. Half of bloody Sydney's trying to get out on this road.'

'Want a peach?' said Fiona, reaching inside a brown paper bag. 'No.'

'Rosie? Want one?'

Rose nodded. She let go of the wishing well and cupped her hands. She closed her eyes and found herself thinking of the garden in *Aladdin's Magic Lamp*, how diamonds and rubies blossomed in bushes, how flowers were petalled with sapphires; and when she imagined the fruit catching light and reflecting magic, she felt the sensation of soft, furry skin, the ripe, sweet warmth of flesh against her tongue.

It was dark when she woke. The car was rattling and jolting along a bush track. Rose sat up and rubbed her eyes. The car's dim headlights lit up the scrub edging in across their path.

Fiona turned in her seat. 'Well, good evening Sleeping Beauty.'

Rose blinked several times. 'When are we going to get there?'

'Soon.' Didi steered the car into the left fork of the track. 'Real soon.' Rose yawned and realised she'd never been to a festival before. She wondered what to expect. Festival, festive, fiesta: celebration. But what were they to celebrate? Australia Day?

Rose closed her eyes and imagined streamers: blue, pink, yellow, orange, tangled up together like when a ship leaves a dock. She saw confetti, a flock of balloons, a marching band with golden tubas and trumpets so bright she could see her face in them. She saw a gypsy shrouded in sequinned velvet, a red silk scarf eloping with a breeze, a stiltwalker with ten-foot legs wearing candy-striped pants. She could almost taste a lick of sugary, pink fairy floss melting in her mouth when the car swerved into a driveway and stopped.

From a one-storey building on their left they could hear the muffled sound of voices, a guitar, and a dog barking. They got out of the car. Rose saw how the ground sloped down ahead of them, where a campfire glowed in the darkness.

'This is it?' she asked, trailing along behind them.

'This is it.' Didi walked up two wooden steps to the doorway of the building. Fiona followed, and Rose stepped in last.

She saw long wooden trestles and benches that measured the length of the huge room. Several bulletin boards were attached to the walls. She saw food being served from large iron pots on a counter nearby. She could smell the thick aroma of bar-b-que chicken, but as she hovered behind Fiona the smells, the colours, the minor chords of the guitar paled under the image of all the women that filled the room.

Some sat in a circle on the floor, singing. Another two stood by a coffee urn, one stroking the other's straight black hair. Didi was already in the arms of a woman wearing only a pair of cut-off jeans, her breasts hanging so low they swung when she moved. Rose hung back as Fiona danced around a nearby trestle and hugged a woman whose nose was pierced with a gold sleeper.

Rose noticed another bare-breasted woman as she hovered in the doorway: a blonde woman biting into a piece of chicken as she walked across the room was wearing only a pair of green army shorts. She's got hardly *anything*, Rose thought, as she stared at the pair of tiny breasts and the small, pink nipples.

The loud, collective chatter blended together, drifted, and hung in the air like smoke. Rose noticed how many women had the same crew-cut hairstyle as Didi; others had short hair at the front and long at the back. Rose even noticed two bald heads, one of which belonged to a woman who was blowing smoke rings into the face of the other.

Rose thought it looked as if they were all related, as if she were witnessing the reunion of some enormous family, a family of some three hundred or so, engaged in the embrace of food and celebration. A sense of warmth and kinship connected them: a head on a shoulder, a hand on a knee. In the centre of the room two women were trying to waltz, the smaller one standing on the feet of the taller as she moved, laughing. It felt like a Christmas party, a wedding reception, a twenty-first birthday. Yes, Rose thought, it did feel like a family, a family with scores of second cousins and many in-laws. A family without husbands, fathers, brothers, or sons.

She lay on the top bunk of a long, narrow dormitory off the main room and wondered what her mother would think: half-naked women, bald heads, kissing. She wondered what the girls at school would think. She should have stayed at the shelter. She shouldn't have come. It was hot. She couldn't sleep. Outside, the cicadas' high-pitched chant counted the seconds away. Mosquitoes buzzed around her in the darkness. She didn't even know where she was. Fiona and Didi had gone down to the campfire to visit friends.

'*Lezzo*,' she remembered. That's what the kids at school call you when they hate you, or just want to make you feel bad. Lezzo, bitch, dickhead, poofta, arsehole. They were all the same. You could put a 'bloody' in front of it and make it sound even worse: *bloody* bitch, *bloody* dickhead, *bloody* lezzo. The boys liked the lezzo one the best.

'C'mon, love!' Rose heard. She felt someone shaking her. It was Flo. Rose was relieved. Flo worked part-time at the shelter. But she wasn't like the others. Flo was old, at least fifty. She was fat, too, with curly, shoulder-length brown hair, thick glasses, and a mole on the right side of her chin. Rose thought Flo was more like a real woman, a mother. Flo even had kids of her own.

'Better get up and get your breakfast before they close the kitchen.'

Rose yawned. 'All right.'

'And when you go up to get it,' added Flo, 'just tell 'em you're with the shelter. OK?'

Rose nodded and reached for the faded yellow dress that she had hung on a hook near the bunk, the dress that she'd found a few days before in the donations bin at the shelter.

After breakfast, Didi asked Rose if she'd like to take a walk down to see the river, and soon Rose found herself shadowing a group of women as they strode along the grassy slope and onto a hard, dry track that wound downward through the bush. It was flanked with ringbarks oozing sap, bleeding under the heat of the mid-morning sun. Rose couldn't see beyond the edge of the track; the pale greens, browns, and greys of branches and bush were thick and impenetrable.

Dried leaves and twigs cracked under their feet and the sweet, pungent scent of eucalyptus hung in the air. As the women chatted she listened to the sudden cry of a kookaburra, though it sounded more like a laugh than a cry. Rose fancied it was laughing at her.

It was when the track curved left and edged around a large sandstone boulder that she saw the mass of clear water flowing eastward and a few heads bobbing up and down in the water. She wished she'd brought her swimming costume. She kept on wishing this until she saw a group of naked women picnicking on a flat rock at the edge of the water.

Didi and the other women jumped down onto the rock. Rose hung back, fiddling with her charm bracelet as she gazed at each shaded of bare skin.

Backs and shoulders were reddening in the sun, arms the colour of copper two-cent pieces, legs as pale as eggshells. Some lay on their stomachs with their white buttocks smiling up at the sky, others were on their backs, with breasts sinking under gravity's beckon. It was a collage of colour, shape, and size. A patchwork of flesh.

'C'mon, Rosie,' cried Didi. She was already slipping out of her overalls. Rose watched her peel off her cheesecloth shirt and underpants, saw the way her round stomach hung over the thick, black triangle of pubic hair, the way her fair skin seemed to sag.

Rose suddenly felt foolish, standing there in her yellow dress and staring at them all. She drew in a deep breath and jumped down onto the rock, but then didn't know where to sit. Didi was already flapping around in the water. Fiona was lying on a blanket with another woman; her slim, olive-skinned body shining with suntan oil.

Finding another flat rock nearby, Rose sat down and dangled her feet in the water.

Some festival, she thought. She ran her toes across the smooth river pebbles. Nude bathing. Topless women. She'd heard of that. Nude bathing and wild parties. Streakers. Hippies. Communes. She'd read about it in the *Telegraph*. She looked up. Didi was on her back, floating like a log headed out for sea. Then another woman, a dark woman with thick, curly black hair, waded over to Didi and took her by the ankles. She began pulling her across the surface of the water, stepping backwards and making a droning noise like a tugboat. Didi closed her eyes and abandoned herself to the movements the woman was directing, her arms dragging behind her head like a rudder.

Suddenly, the dark woman let go, and Didi's legs sailed into a V around the woman's waist. They were both laughing. Still floating, Didi's legs locked around the woman's torso. The woman's hands were moving along Didi's hips.

Rose turned away. She hung her head and gazed at her reflection, her round face distorted, disturbed by ripples created by the nearby swimmers.

'Don't you like swimming?'

She looked up. Fiona was standing beside her.

'It's OK,' she replied, looking away.

'Well, why don't you take off your dress and come on in?'

Rose shrugged.

'Shy?'

'N-no, It's —' her bottom lip quivered '— it's too cold.'

Fiona smiled at her before she turned and waded into the water.

Rose realised that no one had ever seen her naked, no one except her mother and Wanda. Not even her cousin, Brendan, had seen her naked, not even when he emptied out his piggy bank and offered ninety-three cents when she was eight.

Around sunset, after she'd had her tea, Rose looked down to find her feet and calves caked with dirt. She found Flo in the dormitory and asked if she could have a shower.

'Of course you can, Rose,' replied Flo. 'Let me get you a towel. I'll show you where it is.'

Flo stood on the wooden steps of the hall and pointed to a small stone structure about the size of a garage away to the right. Rose thanked Flo for the towel and the cake of Lux as she headed down the steps.

She stopped abruptly in the doorway of the shower room and peered inside. It was dim. She could hear the sound of running water. Steam rose in clouds to the ceiling. She stepped inside. There were no doors on the recesses, no curtains, nothing. They were all bathing together, in twos and threes, lathering up each other's backs and sponging shoulders. Rose held her breath and stared. There was an empty recess on her left. She eyed it furtively. She heard someone cry, 'Chuck me some soap.' She headed for the white sink at the end of the room and lowered her head to a single stream of cold water.

Taking the soap, she turned it within her hands, working along her wrist and up her left arm. She rubbed and lathered, up and down as if trying to scrub a bad stain away or erase her very skin. She lifted each foot to the sink and scrubbed and scoured away the dirt.

As she turned the tap off, she found her dress was splattered with water. She began towelling herself dry, noticing two women, one black, one white, showering together in a recess next to her.

She wiped down her right arm. The white woman's hand stroked the length of the black woman's spine. She wiped down her left arm. The black woman's hands slid around the white woman's waist. She towelled the excess water from her dress. Their bodies met as water rained down upon them: a full pink nipple meeting a dark one like a mouth. She wiped her left foot. Their skin was merging. Each a mirror for the other. Rose towelled her inner thighs. A dark hand cupping a white breast. She wiped her neck. Black and blonde were pressing together. She patted her face. She didn't stop until she'd turned towards the door.

By eight o'clock they had settled themselves on the floor of the hall for an open-mike night. A stool and two microphones were set up at one end. Several women were milling around straightening cords and doing sound checks. The usual loud chatter and laughter filled the room. Rose sat on a wooden chair against one of the side walls. She'd eaten spaghetti bolognaise for tea and it kept repeating on her. She knew she shouldn't have eaten so much.

A small, fair woman with dark, short hair sat on the stool. She was hugging a guitar and wore a pair of blue shorts many sizes too big for her. The only way she kept them up was with a pair of brown braces.

'Test, test,' she called, tapping the microphone with her third finger. 'OK!' she announced, strumming the guitar to see if it was in tune. 'Right-ee-o. My name's Mary and I'm gunna start off by singing a song I wrote last month.'

Her left hand slid around the neck of the guitar; she opened her mouth, inhaled, and sang:

Mama says, What you wanna *be* when you grow up
Mama says, What you wanna *be* when you grow up
Mama says, What you wanna *be* when you grow up
Mama, I wanna be gay

I *don't* wanna graduate to the kitchen
I *don't* wanna end up whinin' and bitchin'
I *don't* wanna wait for a wedding day
Mama, I wanna be gay

I don't wanna have a man to lay me
Mama, I'm weird but I'm not that crazy
I want my independence always
Mama, I wanna be gay

I'm gunna bring home a nice young female
I'm gunna bring home a Jenny or Gail
We're gunna play house a different way
Mama, I wanna be gay!

All through the song the women clapped and whistled and, at the end of every chorus, all shouted, 'Mama, I wanna be gay.'

Applause rippled throughout the hall when the song ended. Rose scanned the roomful of women, looking for other kids. There were three. Two were standing down the back, clapping their hands and shouting, 'Ya-a-y . . .' But they were practically babies, Rose thought. Two or three years old. One was still in nappies. The third looked as though she was about five or six. But she still sucked her thumb. And she was sitting in the lap of a woman, her head nestled snugly between the woman's large breasts.

The woman in the big blue shorts switched guitars, announcing that she liked to play the blues on a twelve string. Everyone clapped in time with the beat, everyone except the girl with her thumb in her mouth, and Rose settled back in her chair and asked herself if she'd tell her mother.

She lay in bed that night and wondered how they did it. She wondered if they did anything. She wondered how it felt.

Was it just nude bathing? And touching? Was that it? Kissing. Laughing. Wearing anything you want. Lesbian.

Before Wanda ran away from home, when Rose was about eight or nine, they used to bathe together. They always ended up fighting for more space in the bathtub. Then Wanda began growing blonde hairs between her legs. Rose remembered how Wanda would count them every night: 'One...two...three...four...' When she got up to seven she started bathing by herself.

Rose rolled over and pulled the sheet up to her neck as the full moon peered in through the open window.

The next morning, after breakfast, Rose found herself trailing behind Didi, Fiona, and about eight other women as they strode down the same bush track to the river. But she hung back, taking slow, deliberate steps. Stopping now and then, she collected gumnuts, paused to examine an anthill, or simply gazed into the bush, hoping to see a wallaby.

The women's voices gradually withdrew down the track and left Rose with only the sound of cicadas and the cries of currawongs.

She continued slowly, pretending that it was a long time ago, pretending that she was an Aborigine collecting fruit and berries. Each hard, brown gumnut became a plum, a blackberry, or a rockmelon. Her two side pockets were brimming with fruit by the time she reached the sandstone rock.

She stopped and contemplated following the track around the rock to where they all would be, just like yesterday, and instead turned, her eyes falling upon a narrower track off to the right that wound through trees and headed upstream.

She found herself running. She didn't know why. She ran as if some Tasmanian devil were chasing her. She leapt over fallen branches and small rocks. She felt dry twigs whipping her arms as she raced by. She heard only a biting whirr at her ears.

The track ended at the river's edge about a quarter of a mile upstream. Rose stood, panting, as she surveyed the fine white sand, the lapping water, the emptiness.

She took the fruit out of her pockets and kicked off her sandals.

She stood ankle-deep in the water and remembered it was still a long, long time ago. She *was* an Aborigine. Was born here in the bush. She waded in knee-deep. She shivered. She has never seen a city before, other people. She waded in thigh-deep. She lives on fruit, sleeps in the hollow trunk of a great-grandfather tree. She crossed her arms in front of her and gripped the hem of her dress. She pulled it up. She swims in the river every morning. She pulled the dress over her head. She flung it on a rock.

The sound of knives and forks clicking together, chairs dragging across the linoleum, snatches of conversation; Rose closed her eyes and listened to it all. Words without a context. The crunch of an apple. A plate being scraped. It was the same everywhere. Teatime had its own vocabulary, the language of the hungry.

She spooned pea and ham soup to her mouth, remembering back to when they were all a family, a real family, before Wanda ran away and her father left on that last tour and never returned, before her mother had the string of boyfriends and ended up with the one she had now.

Then they would eat in the dining room of their big, old house. Her mother would serve spinach rolls and rice on heavy, willow-patterned plates, with fresh orange juice and a decanter of iced water. Afterwards, her father would sit at the head of the table and tell jokes while they all sat chuckling over banana bread. Jazz curled around every corner of the house. The records. Her father's blues. Some horn always wailing in the background of every word he uttered.

Back then, they would wash their hands before they sat down, said grace, even used cotton serviettes, silverware so shiny she could see her upside-down face beaming back in a teaspoon.

Rose picked up her knife and looked up and down the long wooden trestle. Didi was biting into a chunk of French bread; Flo was sipping tea; Fiona was chatting with her neighbour; the thumb-sucker was flicking butter at one of the babies opposite.

Didi and Fiona were sleeping in the bottom bunk. Rose lay above in the top one, gazing out the window, looking for the Southern Cross, the quartet of light, the reference point of night.

The woman with the big shorts and the twelve string guitar was playing the blues again in the hall next door. Velvet chords pressed through the wall, the blue notes penetrating. Rose felt them slow her heartbeat and relax her muscles as she closed her eyes. The woman was moaning phrases, scatting sounds of love and loss. She wailed and crooned as Rose heard the bunk creak. The woman built up a steady riff. Rose heard Fiona sigh. The notes were falling over each other like waves. She heard the bunk squeak. The dynamics were rising. Volume and speed. Rose remembered the river. The water between her legs. The freedom of her limbs. She heard Didi moan. A gasp. A whisper. The water had felt like a caress, an embrace. The bunk shuddered. The woman's voice modulated. Rose's skin tingled. Fiona moaned. The strumming skipped an octave. Higher. The fingering was quick and complex. She remembered the way the current moved across her body like the stroke of a hand. The bunk creaked forward, merging with the B-flat shuffle. It was all one rhythm: the strumming, the current, the sighing. The woman was holding the very last note and it vibrated and enveloped them in the darkness; and, as Rose caught a glimpse of the four stars framed by the corner of the window, she thought it was just like the sounds she'd heard from her parents' bedroom those hot, summer afternoons: the moan, the whisper, the croon, the creak, the gasp, the squeak. It all sounded just like love.

9

SOLO

Rose listened to the tinkle of a piano struggling through loud conversations, orders at the bar, and a game of darts near the stage. She heard the way fingers fumbled through chord changes, the occasional wrong note, the way the tempo would speed up on easier passages and slow down on the more difficult ones of 'A Partridge in a Pear Tree'. She sat up straight and craned her neck to see an old, greying man on the tiny stage at the end of the bar.

'Mum? Can I go and play the piano?'

Her mother put down her middy of beer. 'No.'

'But —'

'Rose, *no*.'

'But he —'

'You no make noise now!' snapped George.

Rose frowned at him, at his brown eyes and curly black hair, the gap between his two front teeth. The velvet rooster. He was short for a man. He wasn't even as tall as her Mum. He liked to wear his shirts with the top four buttons undone so everyone could see his chest. He was only thirty-two. He looked even younger; and wherever the three of them went, Rose felt embarrassed.

'But I *know* how to play "A Partridge in a Pear Tree".'

'Rose, sit *down*,' said her mother. 'Now.'

George turned and ordered two beers — a middy and a schooner — and a pink lemonade. Her mother lit up a Viscount and took a long drag. Rose slouched on the stool and gazed at her sandshoes. She slid her hand inside the pocket of her faded red sundress and felt better when she touched it, her secret wrapped up in pink tissue paper.

Rose had never been in a pub like this before. She thought it looked very old. The walls were made of blocks of honey-coloured sandstone, uneven and rough, marked and chipped. At the end of the pub, near the stage, she could barely see, through the crowd, the outline of a carved, stone fireplace.

A roar broke throughout the pub. Rose jumped. The cheers and hoots came from around the dartboard. A group of men cried out and slapped each other's backs, muffling the sound of the piano and snatches of conversations. A hat flew up in the air. The old man stopped playing. Rose could see a hand rise above the crowd and pour a schooner of beer over someone's head.

'Merry Christmas,' said George as he handed her the pink lemonade.

'Happy Easter,' replied Rose, holding up the glass.

'What?'

'Happy Easter.'

'Easter?' said George, frowning. 'You try and make fun of me or what?' His eyebrows narrowed. 'Huh? You try and make me look *stupid*?'

Rose tensed. George was on his feet, glaring at her. 'Huh? You making me look stupid?'

'N-no,' She was already edging her way back on the stool. 'I just...I —'

'She was just playing,' said her mother.

'But it's Christmas! Right?' George grabbed Rose's arm. Some of the pink lemonade spilled onto her leg.

'Y-yes.'

'So say it.' He squeezed her arm. '*Say* it.' He squeezed harder. '*Say* it!'

'M-merry Christmas.'

'And a Merry Christmas to you,' said George, releasing her arm. 'You make fun of me no more, all right?' he added as he sat back on his stool.

Rose nodded. She hadn't tried to make fun of him. She just liked to play with words. She liked to play with words like she often played around with a line of music, her fingers seeking out the alternatives: accents, embellishments, stresses, spaces and fills, making it a language of her own. She often felt, as she played, that certain notes were particular words and that she could string them together to make sentences. Sometimes she'd be sight-reading from her duets book and would add a flourish, a quick fill, and thus felt as if she were contributing to the composition, so it became more like a conversation than a monologue.

Improvise. That's what her father had taught her, and he was a real pianist, a professional. He'd said that one day before he left for good and Rose never forgot it. She then developed a habit of not only improvising on the melody; often, she realised that she had travelled well beyond the tempo, key and time signature, and sometimes looked down to find her fingers hammering out a story about the wilds of Africa or imitating the lonely drone of a didgeridoo washing across an outback plain. She liked to push language. Music language, English language, Happy Easter: who cares?

It was her mother who had insisted on going to that particular pub that night because she wanted to see Rose's brother, Ned. Ned now lived in a room on the second floor of the pub and worked as a mechanic at Better Brakes. She wanted to see him because it was Christmas Eve, so George had driven them from the south western suburbs into Sydney, through town, into The Rocks, to Heroes of Waterloo Hotel.

The three of them sat in a triangle, Rose furthest from the bar. She rested her glass in her lap and turned to see even more people pushing into the already crowded pub. They clustered along the bar and clutched two, five, ten, and twenty-dollar bills, holding them up like a pass into happiness, while two young barmaids — a redhead and a blonde — pulled Tooheys, Fosters, and Old as if racing each other. The stumbling sound of the piano had disappeared entirely. Rose could hear the whine of 'Dead Skunk in the Middle of the Road' booming out of the jukebox and the cries of people ordering drinks.

'Is Ned coming home for Christmas?' she asked.

'What?'

'Ned. Is he really going to come home for Christmas?'

'I hope so.' Her mother ground the cigarette butt into an ashtray. 'Yes, he will. He probably wall.'

Rose closed her eyes and heard the orders overlap, their cries close to bidders at an auction sale.

'Middy and a schooner.'

'Six schooners and six shots of Bundaberg.'

'Got any Cooper's?'

'. . . And can I have some twenny cent pieces for the machine?'

She inhaled cigarette smoke and the yeasty smell of stale beer, the scent of her own sweat and body odour. It was hot and humid. She slid her hands inside her pockets again and hoped her mother would bake a pudding the next day, like she used to, with the old-fashioned sixpences mixed in with the sultanas and dates. Rose liked Christmas just for that, to spoon sweet, custard-coated pudding into her mouth, her tongue seeking out the tiny silver coins.

After curling her feet around the legs of the stool, she closed her eyes once more, and saw a six-foot Christmas tree, a real one, not like the silver and gold ones you buy at Coles and pull out of a box every year and assemble yourself, not like the one they had at home. No, this was a pine tree that smelt so fresh it was intoxicating. She saw that she was trimming the tree, dressing it like she would a doll, adding light, colour, and texture. She saw herself draping green tinsel around it, adding stars, yellow baubles, an angel at the top. Someone — her father, perhaps — was playing 'Silent Night' on the piano. Candles were burning. Beneath the tree were boxes wrapped in bright, multi-patterned paper, wide blue ribbons and bows. She was wearing her white lace dress with pearl buttons. The room glowed with colour in the candlelight.

'Ned!' cried her mother. 'Oh, I thought you'd never get here.' She stood up and hugged him.

Ned laughed. He was skinnier than ever and was sporting a sandy-coloured goatee beard.

'Never *get* here?' he said. 'Mum, I *live* here.'

'Oh, I know. But you know what I mean. Haven't seen you in ages.'

'Yeah, yeah,' he replied, pulling away from her. 'And how are you, Sunshine?' he added, grabbing Rose under the arms and hoisting her up out of the stool. She wrapped her legs around his waist and hugged him.

'Good,' she replied as he kissed her on the forehead. Their eyes met. 'Are you coming home for Christmas?' She raised her eyebrows.

'I don't know. We'll see.' He kissed her again and lowered her back to the stool. He turned to George. They nodded to each other, both said, 'Hi, how're you going.' Both managed a smile.

Ned ran a hand through his ash-blond hair and announced, 'OK, I'm buying the next round.' His hand went for his back pocket. 'Hey, Doreen!' he cried to the redhead. 'A schooner and a —' he turned to the three of them, lowering his voice. 'What are you guys having?'

'Um, a middy,' said Rose's mother, 'and a schooner of Tooheys for George.'

'What about Sunshine over here?'

'She just had a pink lemonade.'

'Well, when I'm buying,' declared Ned, 'she gets a drink, too.' He turned toward the bar again. 'Yeah, Doreen one...no, two schooners, one middy, one pink lemonade. Thanks, luv. And put a cherry in the pink lemonade.'

Ned turned and grinned at Rose. 'You know, Dad's coming downstairs soon.'

'*Dad?*' exclaimed Rose and her mother. George put down his schooner, his mouth still full of beer. His eyebrows narrowed again. He swallowed. He inhaled. 'What?' he said.

Ned was nonchalant. 'Yeah, Dad. He moved in here a couple of months ago. I got him a great little place on the top floor, better than mine.'

George glared at Rose's mother. Rose tensed again. Her mother looked away and lit up a cigarette.

'Did you know he live upstairs?' said George, leaning across to face her.

Her mother tilted her head back and blew out a grey line of smoke. 'No, of course not. Not that *I* care. I don't care where he lives. Couldn't care less.'

George eyed her for a few moments and straightened on his

stool again. The edges of his mouth were tight, his nostrils a little flared. He reached for his packet of Craven A.

'There you go, mate.' Ned parked another schooner of beer next to George's three-quarter-full one. 'Mum,' he added, handing her a middy. 'And one very big, very pink lemonade with one red, juicy, delectable cherry at the top for Miss Roseanna over here. Tell me, Miss Roseanna,' he continued, bowing ceremoniously as he handed her the glass, 'is the lemonade up to her highness's standards? How is the texture? The palate? I've heard 1973 was a *very* good year for Shelley's lemonade.'

Rose giggled. She lifted the glass to her mouth, taking care to stick her little pinkie out as she'd read the English do when they drink tea. Before taking a sip she sniffed the lemonade once or twice.

'Ver-ry good, James,' she joked in a fake English accent, taking care to roll her r's. 'This will suffice.'

Ned and Rose grinned at each other and clinked glasses, then George and her mother raised theirs. George didn't bother to say 'Merry Christmas' again.

'So,' said her mother after a few moments, 'is your father playing anywhere now?'

Ned leaned against the bar, his right elbow resting in a puddle of beer.

'Oh, yeah,' he replied. 'Dad's doing real well. He just put in a trio at The Rocks Push, and he's got a quartet here in the pub Tuesdays and Wednesdays.' Ned nodded toward the stage and the piano.

Rose smiled to herself, slid her hand inside her pocket again, and brushed the tissue paper with her fingertips.

'He play *here*?' said George.

'Bloody oath,' Ned replied. 'And it cooks, too. People brawling to get in the door.'

'He play *tonight*?' George unbuttoned his shirt cuffs.

'Nah, not tonight. Thursdays he's off. You never know, though. He might hop up and give us a tune or two. Hey Mum,' he added, straightening up, 'can I bite you for a cigarette? It's too much of a song and dance to get over to the machine.'

Her mother opened the packet of Viscounts and offered him

one. George rolled up his sleeves. Rose looked into her glass, at the cherry floating amongst ice cubes. She picked it up between her thumb and index finger and popped it in her mouth.

'Mum's going to bake a plum pudding tomorrow,' she mumbled, looking at Ned, 'with sixpences and —' she bit into the cherry '— vanilla custard.'

'Really?' Ned reached for the box of Redheads that sat on top of George's Craven A's.

'Yep. And a double fruitcake too. Aren't you, Mum?'

'Rose don't be silly.' Her mother brushed a wisp of blonde hair away from her forehead. 'You know it takes weeks to make a fruitcake. You have to soak the fruit in rum for at least a month before you even think about baking. How do you think I can do all that before tomorrow?'

'But you said —'

'Luv, I don't have *time*.'

Rose looked away.

'Don't worry, mate.' Ned slid his hand under her chin and tilted her head to face him. 'We're *all* a bunch of fruitcakes, aren't we? Who needs another one?'

They grinned at each other again.

'Fruitcake?' said George, interrupting their gaze. Ned leaned back on the bar and dragged on his cigarette.

'What do you mean, *fruitcake*?' George inclined towards Ned. 'What you mean, we all fruitcake?'

'Well, you know,' he replied. 'Nutty. Mad. Mad as a fruitcake.'

'Like crazy?'

'Yeah. You know, crazy.' Ned smiled broadly.

'So, do you think I'm crazy?' said George sharply, his eyebrows rising as he leaned closer to Ned.

'Well I —'

'Crazy, huh?' he repeated, this time a little louder. 'You think I'm crazy?'

Ned stepped back a pace closer to his mother.

'No, mate, no,' Ned replied. 'I was, um, I was just making a joke. You know, trying to cheer up Sunshine here. I ah...' he scratched the back of his left hand. 'I wasn't having a go at you or nothing. You know —'

'You no think I'm crazy?' said George, tilting his head to the right as he stared at Ned.

'Course not.' Ned forced a laugh. 'No. No way. You're one of the sanest blokes I've ever known. You know? Straight down the line. Fair dinkum.'

George leaned back and straightened himself on his stool. 'You right.' He picked up the schooner Ned had bought him. 'And I'm smart,' he added, drumming his left index finger against his temple. 'I'm smart too.'

'Right,' said Ned, nodding. 'I bet you...I *know* you are.'

He nodded again. Rose felt muscles in her neck, tighten. They fell silent, each avoiding the other's eyes. Rose gazed into her glass as if it were a crystal ball, hoping for something more, a change, a re-shuffling, an answer, but all she saw were tiny pink bubbles that rose to the surface and burst.

The dart game stopped as more people squeezed into the pub. Doreen shouldered her way through the crowds and closed the doors of the dartboard cupboard when a quarrel broke out between two men, one of whom was threatening to use the other's eye as a target.

An extra barmaid — an older woman wearing a string of pearls over a pale-pink angora jumper — joined the other two in the race to pull beers. Rose noticed that the more people drank the louder they spoke, as if competing with each other for volume. Her mother was beginning to slump on her stool and rested her left arm on the bar for support. Then, as if catching herself, she took a deep breath, straightened her back, and crossed her right leg over her left, the split in her knee-length black skirt exposing her slender thigh in tan pantyhose.

George was trying to engage Ned in a conversation about cotter-pins and difs, but Ned was mostly nodding and looking away towards the front door. Rose moved her stool closer to Nancy while people bumped and pushed against her as they passed or ordered drinks.

Suddenly, above the loud monotone of chatter and laughter, Rose heard the melody of 'Mood Indigo' cutting through the crowd. The notes were like beads of sweat, falling from something bigger and harder, pushed into runs that turned and answered chord changes like a subtle compliment. And there were spaces, too, holes in the sound left wide enough to fit your heart into; and Rose found herself there, somewhere between B flat and F, the progression pulling her beyond the night's clumsy pace.

She recognised a turn of phrase as she would her own face in the mirror, familiar as breath and sunlight, as night and day. She was on her feet, elbowing her way through the crowd, through blankets of smoke and rhetoric, the sound pulling her as if she were a charmed snake.

She found him alone on the platform, hunched over the keyboard, intent as a surgeon at an operating table. He broke into double time, the fingers on his right hand darting between black and white, negotiating time and timbre.

He had his back to her, but she could see he was wearing a pair of jeans, white T-shirt, and thongs, his ash-blond hair, like Ned's, falling into waves and curls.

Rose lifted her right leg and crept onto the platform. She was behind him, gradually taking quiet steps forward. The notes were growing louder, shaping themselves into a run that beckoned her to take another half-step. She was close enough to see the pattern his fingers had fallen into, choreographed in an instant, barely kissing the keys before leaving them. She was close enough to smell a trace of his sweet aftershave, close enough to touch. She hadn't seen him in eighteen months. She was waiting for her moment.

Together. They were inside the sound together. She lifted her right hand. He was working, working his way out, working his way out of a riff. His right hand reached for a detour, another journey. Rose found her moment, felt her fingers touch the keys, replacing her father's hand, taking his detour, his fork in the melody. Their eyes met as she took a run up the keyboard. She saw the way his features rose into recognition, the lines in his face rearranging into rapture. He continued to comp with his left hand. She heard him cry out, say something, her name perhaps, but it all blended with the music as she slid down next to him on the stool.

Together, they were finding their way through the remainder of

'Mood Indigo', each anticipating the other's next phrase. He played the bass line with deep, round tones while she tip-toed through the higher notes of the melody. She remembered how dynamics weighed upon the heart as she knitted tension to the spaces he left. He slid his free hand around her waist and squeezed her.

She then heard him stop abruptly at the end of a chorus and, taking her cue, she edged into a four-bar break, hesitating a little, as if she were afraid of the sound of her own voice. With each measure, she struggled to find the sounds, the sounds to tell him, to tell him how she felt, how much she missed him. Her hand lifted after the fourth measure as she heard him walk into his break. He struck the keys with confidence, not playing too much, reassuring her. And thus their conversation continued, from nuance to implication, from call to response, a question mailed in an overtone and answered in a flourish.

Their laughter pealed around them as they both finished together. His arms were around her. Everyone in the pub was clapping. She felt his kiss on her forehead, heard his questions. She buried her head in his chest and slid her arms around his waist. When she opened her eyes he was still there, holding her.

'OK,' announced her father as he stood at the bar shaking George's hand, 'it's my shout!'

He turned to Rose's mother. 'Nance, what're you having?'

She uncrossed her legs and paused.

'C'mon,' persisted her father. 'Anything you like. I'm buying. Just name your poison.'

'Oh, all right,' she replied, swaying on her stool. 'I'll have a scotch. Johnny Walker Red.'

'George? What about you, mate? Just name it.'

George hesitated.

'C'mon!' continued her father. 'Now, I haven't seen you guys in probably a couple of years. And it's Christmas. So just name it, George.'

George squeezed the half-empty schooner glass he was holding and then looked up.

'Scotch,' he said. 'I have scotch also.'

'Scotch it is.' Her father turned. 'Ned? You having a scotch, too?'

'No way. Gimme a Toohey's,' he replied, 'with a shot of Green Ginger Wine.'

'Coming up,' he declared, and turned towards Rose. 'And what about Count Basie over here?'

Rose giggled. 'A packet of twisties.'

'A packet of twisties!' exclaimed her father. 'One shot or two? Overproof or underproof?'

Everyone began to laugh, even George.

'Straight or on the rocks?'

'Just a plain packet of twisties.'

'Right, your honour,' he replied, nodding, 'coming right up.'

He waved a twenty-dollar bill in the air and immediately the barmaid with the pearls stopped wiping down the bar to dash over to him.

'Hello, Darling,' he announced. 'How are you this evening?'

'Fine thank you, Lenny,' she replied, looking down shyly.

'And may I say that you look *ravishing* this evening!'

'Ohh.' She let out a nervous laugh, and smiled.

'But you always do, don't you? Now let me see,' he continued, folding the twenty-dollar bill in half. 'What we need is two scotches — Johnny Walker Red — errh...a schooner of Toohey's with a shot of Green Ginger. A packet of twisties and two double Jim Beams with Coke. OK?'

The barmaid nodded and began pulling a beer.

'*Two* double Jim Beams?' said her mother, reaching for her packet of Viscounts. 'You're drinking *two* doubles at a time now?'

'No.' Her father shook his head. 'I'm not *that* far gone. The other one's for Liz.'

'Liz?'

Rose shifted on her stool.

George straightened up, suddenly looking interested.

Ned sighed and turned to face the bar.

'Yeah, Liz. Here she comes now.'

Rose watched as he turned to his left and nodded to a young, dark-haired woman dressed in a pale blue miniskirt and white blouse, shouldering her way toward them. Rose wished she could simply lift a finger and rub the image of Liz away, but Liz just kept moving closer.

'You must be Rose.' Rose felt a light stroke of fingers on the back of her head. She looked up and saw long, black eyelashes, mauve eyeshadow, hazel eyes, a smile shaded with pink lipstick.

'Yes,' she replied, looking away.

Her mother swallowed a mouthful of scotch and eyed Liz. George, too, gazed at her and smiled back. Ned was looking down, biting the nail on his thumb. Somewhere near the stage a group of men were shouting 'Skoal! Skoal! Skoal!' And a jug of beer was held up in the air above the sea of heads.

'Liz,' her father went on, looking over at Rose's mother, this is my erhh —' he licked his lips '— this is Nancy. And George. And, well, you've met Rose.'

'Pleased to meet you all,' said Liz, nodding agreeably.

Rose looked across to see her mother force a weak smile.

She could feel sleep wanting to take her away. Head bowed, she wrapped her ankles around the legs of the stool again and closed her eyes.

She heard her mother say, 'So, Liz, you're an air hostess?'

'Flight attendant. They call us flight attendants now.'

'Oohh, flight attendant. That must be interesting, to travel and everything.'

'Yes, yes it is.'

'What's your favourite place?'

'Well, I have to say Fiji.'

'Fiji?'

'Yes. Actually we were on a flight to Fiji when I met L —'

'Lenny? You met him on a plane?'

Rose opened her eyes. Liz nodded. The two women were sitting together at the bar. Liz had slipped off her white pumps. Her mother offered her a cigarette. Liz accepted, then rummaged through her white leather purse. Pulling out a black and silver cigarette holder she said, 'It's the tar. You know, hard on my lungs.'

115

Rose looked up at the old-fashioned wooden clock above the bar, watching the gold pendulum swing back and forth, marking time. It was ten-thirty-seven. She was used to this, a night at the pub, lemonade, twisties, a Sergeant's meat pie, perhaps.

She switched to the other conversation, to her father, George, and Ned, who were clustered together a few feet away, Ned leaning on the bar, the other two sitting.

Her father was saying, 'Tours? Yeah, I've done tours. Plenty of them.' And he placed his glass on the bar for emphasis. 'But I tell you what, George, it's not all beer and skittles.'

'What?'

'Beer and skittles. You know, fun and games. It's not as good as you think.'

George nodded.

'For example, the food. Food's terrible on the road. And the driving. You work all night and drive all day.'

'I like to drive.' George, reached into his back pocket for his wallet.

'Yeah, well, that's probably why you're a mechanic and I'm a muso.'

'I don't know about that logic, mate,' said Ned. 'I'm a mechanic and I *hate* driving.'

'You're not a mechanic,' her father retorted. 'You're a bass player. Remember that. You just fix a few brakes on the side.'

George took out a ten-dollar bill and stood up.

'But hang on.' Her father pulled on George's shirt sleeve. 'I haven't finished.'

George folded the note and sat down again.

'The *worst* thing about being on tour is the pianos.'

George crossed his arms. 'The pianos?'

'Yeah. Terrible. Bloody awful. All those rinky-dink, broken down pianos. All out of tune. What I can't figure is this, a guy buys a nightclub and spends thousands of bucks on the decor. Y'know, doing it up?'

'Renovating?' said George.

'Yeah. Like, remodelling. Bloody wallpaper and spinning balls. All that crap.' Her father downed the dregs of his glass. 'So he reckons all these decorations are going to bring the customers in.

Doesn't spend *anything* on the piano. Just the same broken-down one that's been there for years. And it doesn't make sense, you know?'

George nodded and went to stand up again.

'So do you know what I do now?'

George sat down again.

'When I go into a club and find a piano like that, and have to play it all night, all out of tune and rusty, well, what I do is, after the gig, I take my pair of wire cutters and cut the bloody strings before I leave. That way, they *have* to get a new piano. And then I know I've done a favour for the next pianist that comes along.'

Her father laughed. George looked at him solemnly.

'You not get caught?' he said.

'Nope!'

George frowned and stood up again, shaking his head.

'Dad?' Rose tapped him on the shoulder. He turned and slid an arm around her shoulder. 'Dad, I bought you a Christmas present.'

'You did?'

'Yes. But I didn't know where to send it.'

'Well, you know now,' he said, squeezing her arm.

'Yes, I know. But well, what I was going to do —' she wriggled up closer to him, '— I was going to give it to Ned to give to you. I have it here.'

She touched the lump protruding from the right pocket of her dress.

'Well, now you can give it to me personally.'

'No.' She stroked the golden hairs on the back of his neck. 'Not yet. It's not Christmas yet. We have to wait till twelve o'clock. OK?'

Her father pushed her back gently and gazed at her. 'But I might turn into a pumpkin by then!'

She giggled and fell into his arms again. 'Not until twelve. And Ned's going to come home for his presents, aren't you Ned?'

Ned shrugged and grinned at her. 'Yeah, I guess so. Looks like I don't have much choice.'

Both Ned and Lenny laughed. Rose looked across at George. He had been trying to order the next round of drinks, as were so many other people hovering at the bar like moths at a lightbulb.

Rose noticed George cried 'Hello, darling,' to the older barmaid, as her father had, but she seemed not to hear, and sailed past him on her way to the cash register.

'Excuse me,' he called to another, holding up the bill, but she was busy topping up a pint of Guinness.

The third barmaid, Doreen, wiped down the bar quickly and emptied two ashtrays.

'Who's next?' she asked, looking up.

'Three schooners of Old,' announced a man, about forty or so, whose pot belly bung over his black leather belt.

'Two scotch on the rocks, two double bourbon —' interjected George immediately, holding up his bill.

'Listen, mate,' said the big man, turning. '*I* was next.'

'Bullshit. I wait longer than you.'

'Fucking crap that you did.'

'I fucking did, fatso.'

'You calling me a liar, wog?' The man wrenched George's collar and twisted it round his throat.

'You don't call me wog?' shouted George, pushing him back. 'Bastard! Fucking Aussie bastard!'

George was about to take a swing at the man when Ned caught him by the arms and pulled him back. At the same moment her father leapt off his stool and wedged his way between George and the other man.

'OK, guys,' he said, 'no use having a little tiff over something like this, eh?'

'The wog here was getting pushy!' cried the big man.

'Don't call me wog!'

'Now, now, gentlemen,' said her father, 'I think we can take care of this. Hey Libby,' he called to the older barmaid, 'could you serve my mate here?' He gestured to George. She nodded and asked him what he would like. 'And you,' added Rose's father, turning to the big man, 'you've got Doreen all to yourself. OK?'

The man grunted and mumbled something under his breath.

George handed everyone their drinks without a word. Rose's mother and Liz had turned to face the men, and they sat for a few awkward moments, glancing at each other, stirring their drinks with swizzle sticks. Liz crossed and uncrossed her legs; Rose's mother's eyes fell upon the floor; her father drummed the edge of the bar with his fingertips. Rose watched them all.

'Did you know,' announced Ned, finally, 'that this is the oldest pub in Australia? Did you know that?' He looked at his mother, then at George, then Rose. The three shook their heads. 'Well, it is. The oldest pub. What about that, eh? See those sandstone blocks?' He pointed to the wall opposite the bar, rough and chipped. 'Well, the convicts cut that stone from around the corner, in Argyle Place, and dragged 'em 'round the corner to build this pub. And that's not all,' he added and gulped down a mouthful of beer, chasing it with a couple a quick sips of Green Ginger Wine. 'Down in the basement — the owner showed me one day — down in the basement there's this tunnel. Fair dinkum! I'm not having you on. A tunnel. I've seen it. And it's got little tracks on the ground — like little railway tracks — that run along through it.'

Ned paused and leaned on the bar. 'Now, I must admit the tunnel's caved in in places, and it's too dangerous to explore, but I *do* know where it goes.'

He paused for effect, looking at everyone, waiting for someone to ask 'where?' And it was Rose who asked. She was on the edge of her stool, ready to demand to be shown the mysterious tunnel.

'Circular Quay,' said Ned. 'Where all the boats and ships dock in. The owner's studied all the bloody history books. And do you know *why* the tunnel goes down to the Quay?'

Rose bit her lip. 'Because that was a way for the convicts to escape and sail away and be free forever.'

Ned grinned. 'Nope. What they used to do is, well, you know, everyone would be in here boozing it up and they'd wait until they got a bloke really pissed, you know, completely plastered. Then they'd take him down to the basement, knock him over the head, dump him in a trolley, and push the trolley along the tracks. It's downhill all the way to the Quay. Next morning, the bloke would wake up on a ship, fifty miles out at sea. They used to *shanghai* them.'

'Really?' Rose's mother tilted her head back and blew out a stream of smoke. Ned nodded. 'And you've actually *seen* this tunnel?'

'Absolutely. Two months ago.'

'I tell you what,' chuckled her father, 'it wouldn't help your hangover any, would it?'

'Mum,' said Rose, taking her mother's hand, 'can I go see the tunnel?'

'No.'

'Oh, *please*. Just a look?'

'Rose, *no*. That's all we need, you disappearing down a tunnel and a boulder caving in on top of you.'

Rose sighed and then realised that since George had sat down, he had been completely silent and expressionless, his entire body falling into a kind of corporeal frown that centred itself around the drink he rested on his lap.

There was another awkward lull in the conversation and Ned excused himself to go to the toilet.

'Mention my name,' cried her father, as Ned began to squeeze through the crowd, 'and you'll get a good seat!'

Rose giggled and slid her hand into his. He took a gulp of bourbon, wiped his mouth with the back of his free hand, and announced, 'You know, I think this is great!' He gestured to them all sitting in a rough circle. 'Us all being here together and not getting hung up. And being able to have the kids here. And everyone getting along fine. This is the way it should be.' He picked up his drink. 'Here's to not getting hung up at Christmas!'

Rose's mother and Liz raised their glasses; George reluctantly raised his, too, but instead of simply taking a sip, he drank the glassful down.

Placing his glass back on the bar, her father went on. 'Did I ever tell you about the time when Nance and I first got married and...'

Rose looked at him. He seemed to be addressing everybody.

'...it was our first Christmas being married and everything. Remember that Nance?'

Her mother broke into laughter and swayed a little on her stool. 'Oh, yeah,' she replied, shaking her head, 'the Bösendorfer.'

'Yeah.' Her father began chuckling. 'The Bösendorfer.' He

glanced from George to Liz. 'See, when we first started going out together, I used to say, "Gee, I'd love a Bösendorfer. Nothing's got a tone quality like a Bösendorfer." And I used to rave on and on like that, you know.'

George glared at Rose's father. Liz bit on an ice cube and looked away. Rose wished he would shut up and not tell the Bösendorfer story, but he and her mother just kept on laughing and he continued.

'So we tied the knot in September or August or something.'

'October,' corrected her mother.

'Yeah, well, something like that. And we'd put a down payment on a little two-storey terrace down in Woolloomooloo. It was a pretty rough joint, but, you know, it was clean and cheap, and we were going to do it up.

'So when we moved in — I think it was about a week before Christmas — and Nance is running around putting up curtains and stuff. And there was this one room — I'll never forget it — upstairs at the back of the house. It had an old, marble fireplace and lots of windows and every day before Christmas, Nance'd be in there polishing the floor and cleaning everything. She wouldn't even let me put anything *in* there. She kept saying "Wait until Christmas. Not until Christmas".'

They both started laughing again. Rose's father sipped his bourbon. George lit up a cigarette and dragged heavily, not looking at them. Liz crossed her legs again. 'So what happened?' she prompted.

'Well, come Christmas Eve, this huge truck arrives out the front. And what's on it? A grand piano — a Bösendorfer! I couldn't believe it. And Nance says, real casual, "Oh, yeah, I bought it with my *dowry money*." Can you believe that? Bought it with my dowry money...It was second hand, of course. She'd copped it at an auction sale.

'So, anyway, the bloody thing is so big we can't get it up the stairs. The delivery guys had to drive it round the back lane, hoist it up to the second storey with ropes, over the balcony, and through these French double doors. So Nance and I are standing out in the lane watching them; and they just get the thing over the balcony and through the doors. So we decide to walk around

121

to the front of the house and go upstairs to position it when we hear this KABOOM, a huge bloody crash, felt like a bloody earthquake or something. So we run in through the front door and there's the Bösendorfer, part of the fireplace, bloody plaster and bricks and shit everywhere. It'd fallen right through the floor and into the livingroom!'

Her mother and father broke out in laughter again. He was wiping tears from his eyes and she was holding onto her stool with both hands. After rubbing her eyes, Rose noticed Liz managed a short giggle, but George remained unmoved.

'What about the men upstairs?' said Liz. 'Were they all right?'

'Oh, yeah,' replied Rose's father. 'Oh, they were a bit shaken up. But Nance broke out a bottle of scotch for them and they were dancing out of the house by dawn.'

Rose yawned and touched the lump inside her pocket. Glancing up at the clock, she saw that it was eleven-twenty-five.

'What's so funny?' said Ned as he brushed up beside Rose.

'The Christmas story.' Her mother blew her nose on a cotton hanky. 'You know, the Bösendorfer.'

'Oh, *that* story, Jesus,' muttered Ned. 'Every year the piano gets bigger and the crash it made when it fell gets louder. Hey Dad,' he added, lowering his voice, 'I just bumped into Squeaky in the dunny, and he said he'd meet you in his car in a few minutes, outside his joint. He said it'd be fifty. OK?'

'OK,' replied her father, standing up. 'I'll wander up there now.'

'Can I come?' Already Rose was sliding off the stool and slipping her hand into his again.

'Um, no, Rose. I'll only be a couple of minutes. I just got to go and meet a guy.'

'But I won't get in the —'

'Listen, Rosie,' he said, leaning down and kissing her on the tip of her nose, 'I'll be back in five minutes. OK? I need you to make sure no one pinches my stool. Five minutes, not a moment longer.'

Rose looked at the stool and considered this. 'You promise?'

'Promise.'

'Cross your heart and —'

'Yeah, yeah. All that stuff.'

She squeezed his hand and let go.
'All right.'

Liz had slipped into her white pumps and followed Rose's father out the door, while Ned disappeared into the lounge to play a game of pool.

The three of them sat in a triangle again, George gritting his teeth and taking alternating sips of Tooheys and scotch, his shoulders hunched as he slouched on the stool. In his left hand he fingered his ring of keys, the metal clicking and jangling.

Rose rested a hand on her father's stool and looked around, noticing a woman with a rose tattooed on her right upper-arm staggering by. She made her way out the door — a schooner of beer still in her hand, while two men followed.

A group of people were up on the stage in a line, arm-in-arm, singing 'Jingle Bells', and trying to do the can-can; they mumbled through forgotten lines as the thunder of their feet hitting wood echoed throughout the pub.

George looked up and glared at Rose and her mother. He squeezed the filter of his cigarette between his thumb and forefinger until it flattened. He then picked up an empty glass ashtray from the bar and leaned closer to them.

'See this?' he said through his teeth, holding the ashtray up in his right hand, glancing from Rose to her mother. 'This Lenny's face.' George's lips tightened as he lowered the cigarette to the ashtray and ground it into the glass.

Rose gripped the side of her stool, stunned. She felt blood draining from her face, the thump of her heart marking time.

Her mother said nothing.

George then dropped the ashtray onto the carpeted floor. 'Bastard,' he muttered. 'Rotten bastard.'

Rose bit her lip and tried not to cry, tried not to say anything. It only made it worse. It always did. She flexed the muscles in her arms, thighs, and calves. She had to hold it in.

'I'm no fucking wog!' he cried, stamping his fist onto the bar. 'I'm better than *him*. He's a fucking mongrel. Your father,' he hissed, turning directly to Rose, 'is dirt. No, shit. He's shit. Caca. He's dog shit. You understand?'

She eyed the clock. Ten minutes to twelve. He hadn't come back.

'Look, George,' said her mother, pointing an angry finger at him, 'don't start now. Not here. Shit, do you have to mess up everything? Even Christmas?'

Suddenly, George was still, the barest movement coming from the narrowing of his eyebrows. The lines in his forehead deepened as he grimaced; his fingers gradually curled inward, into a fist, as if trying to squeeze blood out of his hands.

'Go and get Ned,' he muttered to Rose. 'And then we go.'

She looked at them both, too scared to move. His fists were still clenched.

'Go!' barked George, causing Rose to jump. She slid off the stool and began to push through the crowd, brushing up against the backs of strangers. Inside, somewhere in the centre of her body, she felt herself contracting, as if trying to stifle a current or wave pushing up from within.

When she returned holding Ned's hand, George was already on his feet, ready to go. He was straightening his shirt and tucking it in at the back. Her mother was slipping her cigarettes into a gold lamé purse.

George said nothing, just walked straight towards the door, followed by her mother, then Ned. As Rose turned to follow them she glanced at her father's empty stool.

When she stepped through the doorway and out onto the street, into the warm night air laced with a faint scent of salt water, she heard loud cries break throughout the bar. People were hooting and shouting. A whistle was blown. The piano chimed. The voices overlapped one another: 'Merry Christmas'.

Ned slid an arm around Rose when George swung the car left into Argyle Place. The car screeched. Her mother straightened herself and held onto the dashboard. Rose snuggled up next to Ned in the back seat, her feet resting on George's toolbox.

'Jesus, mate,' said Ned, 'take it easy, will you?'

George said nothing, but simply stepped on the accelerator, the white, 1968 Holden groaning under the speed. He drove around the Quay and into Pitt Street, careening through intersections magnetised by the road. Rose felt her heart thumping again, and was only reassured by Ned's arm around her, the warmth of his skin against hers.

'George,' cried Ned again, 'will you slow bloody *down*.'

'Shut up.'

Rose gripped Ned's thigh. The car swerved right into Park Street, charged for one block, and turned left into George Street.

On the steps of Town Hall a group of people stood in light summer dresses, shorts, sleeveless tops. They held long white candles, the bright yellow flames illuminating their faces like spotlights. Rose caught a snatch of their song as the car speeded by: 'Oh, Come All Ye Faithful'. At least Ned is here, she thought.

'George, *please*.' cried her mother. She was still holding onto the dashboard. 'There aren't even any damn seatbelts in this damn stupid car.'

'Shut *up*.' With his left hand he shoved her mother away.

Rose looked out the window and pretended that the car was still, that it was the movie theatres, shop fronts, and pubs that were flying by. She imagined it all to be an enormous piece of scenery pulled by a speeding truck, just like the ones in the movies. An illusion.

He swung the car into Broadway and cried, 'Fuck this country! Fuck your husband! Fuck your kids!'

A group of people staggered out of a pub and began to cross the street. A woman in a tight red dress was wearing only one high-heeled shoe, bobbing up and down like an emu as she walked; another woman was swinging her handbag above her head like a lasso; the rest were straggling along behind carrying bottles and casks of wine.

They were halfway across the street when George steered the car straight for them. The car shook with speed. Ned screamed 'No!' And, like wild kangaroo, the group jumped and scattered to opposite sides of the street as the car cut through.

'You *are* fucking crazy,' Ned yelled, tightening his arm around Rose. 'That's it!' he continued, inclining toward George. 'Stop the damn car. *Now*.'

George said nothing. He fumbled with some switches and buttons below the dashboard. Suddenly, the windshield wipers began flapping back and forth and one of George's cassettes came on. A guitar and piano accordion hummed through the back speakers. George turned the volume up high.

A man's voice crooned in Arabic in a minor key. It blasted throughout the car, and George began to whine along with him, often tilting his head back and taking his eyes off the road for several seconds.

'Stop the *car*. I want to get out,' cried Ned again.

Rose drummed her fingers against his leg. He can't leave now. Not now. Not him, too.

Ned grabbed the back of George's collar. 'Do you *hear* me?'

George turned and tried to push Ned back with his free hand as the car swerved between lanes.

Rose grabbed Ned's arm and pulled him back. The car began to slow as they approached a major intersection.

She held her breath as she felt Ned's arm slide away, heard the squeak of vinyl as he edged across the seat, saw him pull the door handle and spring out onto the street.

'You coming?' He looked at Rose and she glanced at her mother. In the end it would make things worse. She shook her head. The door slammed and an image of Ned's figure receded as fast as a scene-dissolve in an old movie.

Her mother rolled down her window and called to him, but George had already hit the accelerator again as if nothing had happened and they sped along Parramatta Road, through Stanmore, and into Petersham.

Rose cowered in the corner of the back seat. There were few cars on the road now. They roared past a beer brewery, the closed fruit shops and Italian delicatessens.

George had slowed down to about forty miles an hour, but was taking delight in zigzagging the car in and out of lanes. He cut in front of another Holden and barely missed jamming up against a Volkswagen. Rose doubled over and held her face in her hands, whispering:

Our Father who art in Heaven...
'Stop it!' screamed her mother.

...hallowed be thy name...

'Shut your fucking face!'

...thy kingdom come, thy will be...

'I won't, you mongrel!'

...done, on earth as it is...

'Whore! Bloody whore!'

...in heaven. Give us this day...

Her mother screamed. Rose bolted upright. George's left fist was striking her mother's head as he continued to steer with his free hand.

'Just shut your mouth!' he cried, the blows falling across her face and upper body.

Rose wanted to cry, to scream, her mouth opened but nothing came out. She found herself lifting her arms, her fingers spreading, her hands around his throat. She felt the stubble of his day-old growth, the adam's apple lump, veins against her palm.

She reeled back after his elbow rammed into her face, aware of only a dull ache crawling through her head until seconds later a siren suddenly cried out from behind. A blue blade of light cut through the car. George pulled into the curb and the police parked in front of them.

Her mother was the first to spring out onto the street.

'A knife,' she cried to them as they approached. 'He's got a knife! Book him!'

Rose opened the closest door and jumped out also, relieved to see the two men with their leather boots and holsters. They walked to the right side of the car.

'OK, mate,' said one, peering through a half-open window. 'Out.'

George rolled the window down fully. 'What the matter?'

'Get out!'

'He's got a knife.'

'What *I* do?' mumbled George, opening the door reluctantly.

The policeman wrenched him up by the collar and slammed him against the car.

'For one thing,' said the policeman, frisking him down, 'you're pissed as a fart. Can't even drive bloody straight. We call it driving under the influence.'

'I not drunk.'

'Don't bullshit me —' the policeman began going through George's trouser pockets '— or I'll add resisting arrest to your charges.'

'Found the knife,' declared the other, who had been rummaging around under the front seat.

He held it up: six inches of sharp, shiny metal catching light and glinting, the tip pointing to George like a finger.

Rose stood on the footpath and held her mother's hand as she watched the paddywagon's double doors close in front of the outline of George's frame. She couldn't understand why they were just leaving the two of them there. They said they weren't a taxi service, that it wasn't their job to give people a lift home.

When she heard the engine start, saw the wagon pull away and disappear around the corner, she turned to face her mother, and wondered what they were to do next. The car was useless. Her mother didn't drive. Rose looked up and watched her as she rooted through her purse and pulled out only a handful of change.

'Mum?' Rose glanced up and down the dimly-lit street. 'Where are we?'

'I —' her mother clipped her purse shut '— I don't know.'

'Can we walk home?'

'It's hard to say. I don't know where we are.'

Rose saw that her mother was swaying.

'Come on,' she said, gently pulling her hand. 'Let's go this way.'

She began to guide her mother down the street, leaving behind the sound of the windshield wipers still flapping back and forth. Her mother found it difficult to walk straight as they dawdled past brick houses, a few hedges, and a white picket fence. Rose slipped an arm around her and they managed to walk three blocks before her mother sat down on the footpath beneath a streetlight and vomited, the amber liquid and strings of saliva falling into a tiny pool in the gutter.

'Just let me,' she gasped, 'rest for a few minutes.'

Rose nodded and leant against a telegraph pole. Her mother was bent over, holding her stomach. Straining to see further down the street, Rose noticed, towering above the houses, the poin~ ~f a steeple piercing the sky.

'Wait here, Mum,' she cried, running off before her mother could protest.

She crossed over to the next block and continued running until she found herself facing the two large, wooden front doors of the church.

She took a deep breath and raised her hand, remembering the taste of Holy Bread melting in her mouth, the hymnal chords of an organ, deep purple robes, a golden goblet. She rapped her knuckles against the wooden door and waited.

Nothing. She knocked harder, beat her fist against the door.

Still nothing.

She turned and ran around the side, through a garden, looking for the rectory. She came to a high, concrete wall with an iron, padlocked gate. She held onto the bars of the gate as she peered through, barely able to see the bed of tulips blooming on the other side. Swinging around, she glanced up at the church windows. All was dark but for a faint light glowing from within. The altar, perhaps.

Rose ran back to the front door and again pounded with both hands. She pressed an ear against the wood, expecting to hear the sound of approaching footsteps and the click of the door unlocking.

Stepping back, she lifted her right leg and gave the door one final blow with her foot. She then spun back and began to stride around to the other side of the church only to find, several yards away, a towering pine decorated with bright flashing lights, red glass baubles, silver tinsel and stars. Beneath it were gifts wrapped in purple and white polka-dotted paper with yellow ribbons.

Rose tried to stop, but nothing could suppress the wave she felt pushing through her like a new tide advancing on a beach, blurring shape and line.

She ran towards it and suddenly found herself ripping off the glass baubles and grinding them into the ground with the heel of her shoe. Snatching up a plastic angel, she ripped off its head and flung it into the air. Tinsel was pulled off and strewn across the lawn. She yanked at the yellow ribbons, tore away the paper, and ripped it into shreds, tossing it to the breeze like confetti. She kicked a smaller box into the air and jumped on another. She ran around to the other side of the tree and tore off a foot-long, inflatable Santa Claus, squeezing the fat belly between her hands until it burst.

Out of breath, she dropped onto the grass and lay amongst the debris of broken light and colour. Sliding a hand into her pocket, her fingers wrapped around the gift and drew it out.

Rose sat up, crossed her legs, and peeled back the layers of pink tissue paper one by one until it lay flat in her hand, the miniature, iron organ-grinder. She took the tiny handle between her thumb and forefinger and began to turn. The slow, stuttering melody of 'The Entertainer' tinkered softly around the tree. Nothing else but the rhythm of her own breath met the silence.

JENNIFER MAIDEN
Play with Knives

Play with Knives is a chilling, fascinating exploration of violence, power, morality and grief.

The novel centres around Clare, a young woman shortly to be released from prison. As a child she had murdered a young brother and two sisters.

How was this monstrous act possible? Does the act mean that Clare herself is a monster? As central to the unfoldment of this unforgettable novel is Jennifer Maiden's exploration of the character and motivation of the probation officer, through whose eyes and questions Clare is gradually revealed.

This is a novel which has all the momentum, even the inevitability of a sudden accident, when the observer is appalled, yet utterly transfixed. For after such an event, no line of vision remains unaffected.

MICHAEL STEPHENS
Matinee

'The novel's surface is as quiet and steady as the apparently safe, humming suburb of Sydney's Rose Bay; but beneath it are the powerful reverberations of disintegration, violence, and anti-semitism that affect those the vulnerable Jim loves most...' **Andrea Stretton**

Twelve-year-old Jim lives with his parents and brother in Rose Bay, a Sydney suburb where life should be lived at a smoothly predictable pace. But life is never so tidy, and the disruptions that Jim observes and attempts to understand will be widely recognisable.

An *Australian*/Vogel award finalist, *Matinee* is a novel about isolation told in a communal fashion, engaging readers in enlarging circles as they follow Jim from school to home to neighbourhood, exploring the bizarre incompetence of adult relationships and creating—en route—tender and unexpected insights into the peculiarities of 'family life'.

DAVID OWEN
Coping with Pleasure

David Owen was highly praised internationally for his 1988 novellas, *Eden* and *Venter & Son*:

'Not to mince matters, *Venter & Son* bears, in its stark intractabilities, comparison with Conrad's shorter work.' **Justin Wintle, INDEPENDENT.**

'Owen's work is marked by its restraint, its manner one of allusion and intimation, a flow of events kept in check so that it never obscures the essence of the work, which is the dialogue of narrator and reader.' **Helen Daniel, AGE.**

Coping with Pleasure has not been written with the backing of the Melbourne Tourist Authority—but it certainly presents the city in sharp contrast to the 'staid' image Victorians themselves have long resisted.

Pluto Hartwig and Mintie, his wife, life in up-to-the-minute Melbourne. They are a charming couple and, what's more, in love. Pluto is not entirely happy, but this does not slow his repartee, nor his round of parties and 'events'. Nevertheless, the loss of a beloved Norton, and the fear that Pluto has been academically duped, concern the loving couple and tempt Pluto to despair.

CLAIRE McNAB
Lessons in Murder

Take Detective Inspector Carol Ashton: isn't there something not quite decent about a cop who is quite so good looking, quite so clever, quite so famous—and not even mildly heterosexual?

When a teacher is murdered at a Northern Beaches Sydney school, and when that teacher is the son of a former Premier of New South Wales, only the best cop will do. And, despite her irregularities, Carol Ashton is the very best. But even she does not bank on falling more than somewhat in love with her chief suspect, a charming, attractive teacher named Sybil.

Claire McNab is a Sydney writer. *Lessons in Murder* is the first in a series of suspense novels featuring Detective Inspector Carol Ashton. The second in the series is titled *Fatal Reunion*.